Baggage Claim

Book One
Tru Exceptions series

WRITTEN BY
Amanda Tru

Baggage Claim
Copyright © 2011 by Amanda Tru

Cover design by Susette Williams

Walker Hammond Publishers
ISBN-13: 978-0615625980 (Custom)
ISBN-10: 0615625983
Also available in ebook publication

PRINTED IN THE UNITED STATES OF AMERICA

Acknowledgements:

Special thanks to the exceptional people in my life. To my husband, my parents, Flane and Connie Walker, and my sisters, Cami Hammon and Janna Frazier--whose help and faith made this book possible. To my friend, Samantha Bayarr, whose help and advice has been invaluable.

This, my first book, is dedicated to my parents. I knew that if I ever published a book, it would have to be dedicated to my parents, whose footsteps led me, prayers saved me, words encouraged me, dreams motivated me, and unwavering belief sustained me.

And to Him. Ephesians 3:20

Chapter 1

"We are having some trouble locating your luggage, Miss Saunders."

"I realize that," Rachel replied dryly. "And that is why I'm here at the Lost Luggage counter."

Rachel's bad attitude and impatience didn't seem to register with the dark-haired attendant as she stared at the computer screen with a furrowed brow.

"You came from Helena, Montana. Had a layover in Cincinnati. But neither of those places has record of your suitcase."

This was taking forever! They had already been over all of this! Did this airline send people who couldn't cut it in other departments to man Lost Luggage? This was ridiculous!

She would say that she had the worst luck ever, but that wasn't necessarily the case. She was, after all, here in New York on an all-expense paid trip that she had won through a nationally syndicated talk show.

Rachel glanced nervously at the clock and the front door of the airport. The shuttle to her hotel was scheduled to leave at any time. If she missed this one, she had no idea when another one would be available.

"Look, Stacy," Rachel said, reading the attendant's name badge and trying to get her attention off her computer and on to Rachel's situation. "I'm in a big hurry. The shuttle to my hotel is leaving right now. Can you just have it delivered to me there when you find it?"

"Oh, yes!" Stacy brightened, as if this was a great idea that had never occurred to her. "What hotel are you staying at?"

"The InterContinental at Times Square."

"Great. Okay, let me just run in back and get a form for you to fill out." She quickly scurried through a door.

Seriously? Rachel wanted to beat her head against the counter. To make matters worse, Stacy was gone an exceptionally long time. After impatiently tapping her foot for five minutes and feeling adrenaline course through her veins, Rachel finally sighed and gave up. She knew she'd missed the shuttle. Now she'd have to hire a taxi to take her to the hotel. That pretty penny would definitely not be included in the "free trip."

To make matters worse, Rachel was not the only one waiting. Four other people, probably also with lost luggage, were in line behind her. They were growing increasingly impatient as well, whispering, shifting their weight back and forth between their feet, and sending accusatory glares in Rachel's direction. Rachel knew that, in their minds, she was at the head of the line, therefore any delay must be her fault.

Unconsciously, Rachel began impatiently drumming her fingers on the counter. How long was this going to take? This was her first time in New York, and she really didn't want to miss any of her group's planned activities.

"Excuse me," Rachel felt an insistent tap on her shoulder and turned around to find a strikingly handsome man in line behind her. Under the Wikipedia definition of 'tall, dark, and handsome,' Rachel was sure she'd find a picture of this man.

"I'm sure you drumming your fingers ad nauseam on a counter is considered highly entertaining for everyone back on the farm, but here in the real world, it is considered highly annoying to anyone with an IQ above 40."

Rachel felt her face warm up. She was embarrassed. She hadn't even realized she had been incessantly drumming her fingers. But, she was also angry. He could have been nice about it, but instead he'd just earned the title of "The-Rudest-Man-Rachel-Had-Ever-Met." In the battle between her embarrassment and anger, anger won.

Pointedly, Rachel looked the man over from his dark, wavy hair to his expensive shoes. "Well, sir, if you are the finest male specimen New York has to offer, I think I'll stick with those 'back on the farm.' I'll have to remember to mark in my travel guide that along with some of the tallest buildings, unsuspecting tourists can also encounter The Rudest Man."

"Sweetheart, if you are naive enough to think me intolerable, then you'd better get right back on a plane and go back to the farm where you belong, with or without your luggage."

Now, Rachel didn't feel she'd gain any points by clarifying that she lived on a ranch, not a farm. How did he even know she was from the country? She hated to think it was that obvious. She'd taken pains to dress stylishly, wear her medium blonde hair loose in a current style, and not look as obvious as one of the Beverly Hillbillies.

Rachel opened her mouth to tell the man exactly what she thought of him, but the airline attendant came back through the door with a paper in hand.

"Just fill this out, Miss Saunders, and we'll have your suitcase delivered as soon as possible.

Rachel began filling out the information. She mentally kicked herself for even checking that suitcase. She had wanted to wear something nice to the Broadway show and hadn't wanted to stuff it into a carry-on. But right now, rumpled clothes would be far better than none at all! Stacy went back to her computer, showing no inclination to help the other people in line.

"Excuse me," The Rudest Man said to the attendant. "Do you think you could help someone else while she's filling that out?

"I'm sorry, sir," Stacy replied. "Let me finish with her, and then I'll help whoever is next."

There were obvious groans and snorts of indignation from the others in line. As terrible as it was, Rachel felt a surge of pleasure that the jerk was going to have to wait a little longer.

Finishing, Rachel handed the form back to Stacy. "I'm only in New York for the weekend. Exactly how long is it going to take to locate my suitcase?"

"I'm not sure," Stacy replied, her brow furrowed once again. "I have another guy on a computer back there trying to locate it. Let me just run back real quick and ask him what he thinks."

"No, no!" Rachel tried to protest. The rest of the people in line would probably just lynch her right there if, because of her, the attendant disappeared indefinitely a second time. "You don't need to…"

As Stacy started through the door, a man came through holding something black in his arms.

"That's my suitcase!" Rachel squealed.

The man, unsmiling, came around the counter, plopped the suitcase down beside Rachel and disappeared back the way he came.

"Thank you, George!" Stacy said, beaming at what she probably felt was her own success in locating the missing luggage.

Graciously overlooking the drama and thanking Stacy for her help, Rachel pulled out the handle to wheel the suitcase to the door.

"Maybe you should look inside to make sure everything is there," The Rudest Man offered. "You don't want any surprises."

Stacy bristled. "No one at this airline would ever open a suitcase without serious cause or permission. It's strictly against policy."

"I'm sure it is," The Rudest Man replied. "Nevertheless…"

"This is my suitcase. I'm sure it's fine." Rachel said, addressing Stacy and completely ignoring the man. She was not about to follow any advice from him, if just for the sake of principle. "I'm in a big hurry. I'll look it over when I get to the hotel. If there's anything wrong, trust me, I won't be shy about it."

Hurrying away before she received any more unwanted comments or advice, Rachel went through the sliding doors. She was relieved to see several classic New York yellow taxis parked at a curb. This country girl had never even ridden in a taxi before. Hopefully there wasn't some kind of unwritten protocol, or rules she didn't know about hiring a taxi. Her education on taxis and New York in general consisted of what she had learned from TV shows.

As she walked toward the cars, one of the cabbies jumped out.

"Here, Miss," he said. "I'll stick that suitcase in the trunk for you and then you can tell me where you're headed.

Relieved, Rachel slid into the back seat, told the driver the name of her hotel, and prayed the ride wouldn't cost all of her spending money.

She had been so excited to be one of four lucky winners to win the contest and get to go to New York to see a filming of the sponsoring talk show, a Broadway production, and other tourist destinations. She had always had notoriously bad luck and hadn't won a single contest in her life. Yet, when she had actually won this free trip, she thought her luck had changed. But, after being randomly selected twice by security for full body screenings that seemed to include everything but a blood test, she had been seated on the airplane between two very large men, at least one of which spent the flight passing some very unfortunate and possibly toxic gas. Follow that up with lost luggage and a missed hotel shuttle, and suddenly her luck wasn't looking so good.

Thankfully, other than a few pleasantries, the cabbie wasn't overly talkative. Rachel was glued to the window, feeling very much like a country hick in the city for the first time. She did appreciate the few times the cabbie pointed out interesting landmarks. The ride took longer than Rachel expected, and, when the cab finally pulled up in front of the impressive InterContinental Times Square Hotel, she tried to appear very calm and collected as she handed the cabbie his wad of cash. How could people in New York afford to regularly hire taxis?

Rachel got out of the car, and the cabbie popped the trunk for her to get her suitcase. She lifted it out and stepped to the curb as the cab pulled away.

"Rachel!"

Surprised, Rachel looked up from battling to get her suitcase set on its wheels. Before she could even move, a dark-haired man ran up, grabbed her close, and kissed her passionately on the mouth. Rachel went completely numb, too shocked to even think. He finally pulled away, continuing to hold her close and grin at her like she was the absolute best thing in his life.

"Sweetheart! I'm so glad you're here!" he said joyfully.

Recognition hit. This wasn't a complete stranger. She knew this man! He was 'The Rudest Man' from the airport, only now, he obviously wasn't acting so disagreeable. Indignation rose in her. How dare he! Her hand itched to slap him fully in the face. As if he realized her intention, he blocked her hand and held it firmly in his continued embrace.

Bending close and smiling, he whispered in her ear. "I'm an agent with Homeland Security. If you want both of us to survive the next ten seconds, you'll play along and do exactly as I say."

Rachel's mind was too shocked to put together any reasoning or coherent thought. Her first instinct was to not believe him. As his gaze briefly flickered downward, her own gaze followed. He was holding his badge pressed firmly between their clasped hands. However, it was the urgency in his eyes, and maybe even a trace of fear, that drew her certainty. This man was not lying.

Rachel's thoughts fumbled with confusion and stark terror. Fortunately, her body seemed to take over, switching to a highly competent autopilot.

As the agent released his vise-like grip on her hands, Rachel smiled, reached up, and wrapped her arms around his neck. If her life depended on her playing this part, then she was going to aim for an Oscar.

Rachel was tall, but she had to stand on her tiptoes as she snuggled closer and kissed him lightly.

Responding, he kissed her back, his fingers tangling in her long, wavy hair and his lips seeming to thoroughly savor hers.

Rachel was lucid enough to realize this agent was very accomplished in the art of kissing. She was left breathless and with heart palpitations, which of course she attributed entirely to the danger they were in.

"I'm taking you to dinner right now," the agent said, taking her suitcase in one hand and holding her hand in the other. "You can check into your hotel later."

He quickly urged her into a waiting taxi, sliding in beside her with her suitcase on his lap.

As he shut the door, the driver immediately pulled out and began weaving through traffic.

"We're being followed," the man said. "Sit close and act like we're still enjoying each other."

"Who is following us?" Rachel asked, fighting the urge to turn around and try to spot the enemy. She obediently scooted closer to him and inclined her head towards his.

Instead of answering her question, the agent wasted no time in propping the suitcase on his lap and unzipping it.

"What are you doing?" Rachel demanded. Still, the agent didn't answer

"That's my suitcase!" Even Rachel realized that she was starting to shriek. "Who are you? Would someone please tell me what's going on!"

"My name is Dawson Tate," the man replied simply and calmly as he lifted the lid of the suitcase.

Dawson reached in and moved aside a few of Rachel's clothes and undergarments. Rachel's protests died on her lips. Beneath the top layer of clothes was nestled a complicated looking contraption. The only part she could identify was what looked to be a blank display, like on a digital clock.

Shocked, Rachel stammered, "Is that a… a…?"

Understanding her unfinished question, Dawson answered calmly, "Yes, it's a bomb."

Chapter 2

"What's a bomb doing in my suitcase?" Rachel shrieked, thoroughly freaking out.

"Rachel, you need to stay calm," Dawson ordered, not even looking her direction. "Remember our audience. Keep pretending to be infatuated with me."

Rachel was tense and quiet as Dawson carefully touched and inspected the contraption. Other than the display, it didn't look like a typical bomb you would see on TV. There were no multicolored exposed wires. Instead, the display was mounted on some kind of large metal case. A small screen, about the size of an iPad sat on the case beside the display monitor. Standard looking electrical wires connected the screen to both the case and the display.

After quickly, yet gently inspecting every square centimeter of the contents of the suitcase, Dawson took his cell phone out and pushed a button.

"We've got the girl and the suitcase. It's as bad as we thought, maybe worse. I've never seen a bomb like this before. It's all computerized with the explosives and wiring encased in a box. I can't get into the box, but I'm pretty sure everything is rigged with trip wires so that if you were to attempt to get inside, the bomb would go off. I'm fairly certain that it's also rigged with an internal tracking device. How else would they know when the girl had the bomb in position? I see no clear way to disengage the tracking device or disarm the bomb."

After listening a minute, Dawson said, "I'll do better than that, I'll send you a picture."

Using his phone, he took a picture of the bomb and sent it. His phone rang about twenty seconds later.

"Okay, and you're sure turning the screen on won't trigger it?" Dawson asked. "Alright then, I'll just try not to push the wrong buttons."

As a blue screen came up, Dawson removed a small wireless keyboard from where it had been nestled between the bomb and the side of the suitcase. As he listened and typed for the next two minutes, Rachel had to fight the strong urge to bite her fingernails. Apparently, finding what he was looking for, he rattled off a bunch of letters and numbers that were displayed on the screen.

"Okay, but get it done fast," he said. "We have no idea how strong this thing is or how much patience these guys have. It doesn't matter where in New York we are. If this thing goes off, we're talking about major damage and lots of people dead."

Disconnecting the call, he leaned forward and spoke to the driver in a cheery voice. "Well, Joe, the bottom line is they don't know how to disarm it or even disable the tracking device. We've got to buy them some time while they try to hack in and figure it out remotely. I guess you're our tour guide. It's not like there's a less populated area of Manhattan to take this thing to. We should stay away from Times Square, obviously, since that was the target. We should probably also avoid the Financial District. How does a trip around Central Park sound? That way they'll think we're just doing a romantic sightseeing trip, and if it goes off, the blast won't be entirely absorbed by buildings and people."

"Are you sure we shouldn't head north and try to get it as far away from Manhattan as possible?" Joe asked.

Rachel couldn't help feeling a little surprised that Joe was with Homeland Security as well. He looked to be in his forties and was a smaller man than Dawson. His face had the rough stubble of a few days break from shaving, and a Yankees baseball cap covered what Rachel thought was probably a receding hairline. All considered, he looked the part of a typical taxi driver.

"We can't leave Manhattan until they have the bomb disarmed or at least the tracking signal disabled. The minute the terrorists think it's leaving Manhattan, they'll detonate it. If we even cross a bridge, we're goners."

"Got it," Joe responded. "We're still leading a bit of a parade. I've spotted at least two vehicles who are following a short distance back, but, right now, they don't seem to be insisting on an interview."

Dawson put his arm around Rachel. "Good, maybe we've got them fooled for now, or at least a little off-balance. They don't know who we are and are probably hoping Rachel will eventually make it back to her hotel."

"Why?" Rachel asked, finally feeling like she could interrupt the conversation to get some answers.

"Why do they want me to go to the hotel? What is their plan? Oh, and who exactly are *they*?"

Dawson used his arm to pull her close and touched his forehead to hers. Rachel fought the urge to squirm out of his embrace. Her romantic history was rather sparse. She knew that she tended to be very picky. But, to her credit, the selection in rural Montana was quite slim. Now, having a stranger show more physical affection than Rachel had ever experienced was more than a little disconcerting, despite the necessity. Rachel realized that anyone following them would think the two shadows in the back seat were having a loving and intimate conversation.

"*They* are a group of highly organized, highly intelligent, highly determined terrorists. Their plan was for you to take the bomb in your suitcase into your room at the hotel, at which time they would detonate it."

"But why would they want to blow up my hotel? I would think some tall skyscraper in the financial district during the day would have been the target, like on 9-11."

"There are some high level political figures staying at that hotel right now. They're here for some meetings, but their lodging was supposed to be kept secret. Obviously, the terrorists found out about it. Also, the hotel is the InterContinental Times Square. It's one of the best hotels and located in the heart and cultural center of the city, if not the country. A bomb at that time and location would be devastating economically, politically, and emotionally, not to mention the lives lost and the damage to the morale of the entire country."

Rachel closed her eyes, trying to wrap her mind around this unbelievable, nightmarish situation. It seemed straight out of one of those futuristic disaster movies. And those movies never had a 100% character survival rate.

"But why me? Why was I the mule? I'm from Montana, for Pete's sake! The population of my hometown is less than 1,000, and that estimate probably includes a few cows rather than people! Why would they use me? I'm a nobody!" Rachel groaned and put both hands on her head. "This feels so surreal. I don't understand how *I* could get mixed up in a terrorist plot."

"You were just in the wrong place at the wrong time, Rachel. Or, from the perspective of these terrorists, you were headed to exactly the right place at exactly the right time."

Rachel pinned Dawson with a mildly accusing gaze. "I recognized you as the rude man from the airport. Why didn't you stop me there?"

"I really wasn't that rude. I had a bad feeling about the way things were going. I was kind of hoping, for your sake, that if I made you mad enough, you'd leave or hurry things up and get out of there."

"But if you knew about the plan, why didn't you stop them from putting a bomb in my suitcase in the first place?"

"I didn't know about the plan--at least I didn't know enough details to take any action and risk the consequences. We have been investigating an upcoming terrorist attack on New York City for some time, but we've not been able to identify any of the details of where, when, and who was involved. We just today picked up enough chatter to determine the plot was going forward immediately. From that same information, we suspected the bomb might somehow come through luggage at the airport. We still had no idea of the identity of the persons involved, the target, or the intended time frame. We sent undercover agents throughout LaGuardia, watching for anything suspicious. It occurred to me that the absolute best way to get a bomb in the right place without arousing suspicion would be to have someone unknowingly deliver it. However, I was not the only agent in that line behind you."

As they talked, the taxi wound its way around the Central Park area. Dawson would periodically point at things, trying to provide a pantomime of sightseeing for those observing.

"I guess you did try to get me to open the suitcase there at the airport," Rachel said while trying to match appropriate gestures to Dawson's performance. Under normal circumstances, Rachel's eyes would have been glued to the window, taking in everything that was New York. But, she was currently having trouble taking her eyes off the ominous suitcase bomb still perched in Dawson's lap.

"Yes," Dawson replied. "I thought that if they really had planted a bomb in your suitcase and you started to open it, they would have to somehow tip their hand to try to stop you. Then we could have taken care of the problem there. But you didn't feel like cooperating."

"No, I didn't. In retrospect, I wish I had."

"No, actually, it was probably a good thing you didn't. If we had known for sure about the bomb, all the DHS and FBI agents in the airport would have descended on that suitcase. No one would have come close to disarming the bomb before the terrorists decided a New York City airport was a good enough target."

"But I still don't understand why I was the mule. Were they just waiting for someone who was staying at the InterContinental Times Square to lose some luggage?

"No, we think you were targeted specifically in that regard. The best we can guess is that the company who is sponsoring your trip booked all of your travel arrangements through a travel agency. Those records listing the details of your travel wouldn't be difficult at all to obtain. Your bags were probably 'lost' intentionally so the contents could be replaced."

"So, have you also figured out who the terrorists are? Have they been arrested? Was that Stacy at the Lost Luggage counter one of them? She acted very strange, but I never would have pegged her as a terrorist."

Dawson laughed. "And you think you can spot a terrorist a mile away? The short answer is no. We don't know who's behind this plot. We have some suspects, but we can't make any arrests until we figure out this bomb. Right now they don't realize that we're on to them. The minute we start making specific inquiries and arrests at the airport, this thing blows sky high, literally. But, gut instinct? No, I don't think Stacy is a terrorist. I think she's probably just a pawn like you."

Rachel hated the thought that she had been a pawn. In a lot of ways, she still was. Now it was just the other side's turn to use her.

"So what do you think our chances are? Do you think they'll be able to disarm that thing before the terrorists get impatient?" Rachel asked, still staring at the bomb, expecting it to come to life at any second.

Rachel felt Dawson's eyes on her, as if he were taking her measure and wondering exactly how much truth she could handle.

"Our chances aren't good," he said finally, apparently deciding to be blunt. "This bomb uses new technology we haven't encountered before. If the expert geniuses had enough time, they could probably disarm it, but, at any moment these people could figure out what we're trying to do and blow it up. If you are the praying type, you'd better be making some intense conversation with God. I'm sorry, but it's not at all likely we'll survive this. We don't even know how strong the explosion would be, so we'll just have to do the best we can to minimize the damage. The good news is, if they detonate the bomb, you won't have time to feel anything."

"Oh, good, that makes me feel better," Rachel replied sarcastically. "How could a bomb that fits in my suitcase be such a threat?"

"As I said, it uses new technology, so we're not exactly sure what we're dealing with. If I had to guess, the bomb is using C24 as an explosive. C24 is twenty-five times more powerful than C4. The terrorists are going to be very reluctant to part with it; not only because of their ruined plan, but because C24 can be traced. It's like a fingerprint. If we have the bomb, we have them. But, if this thing goes off, we're talking massive casualties and destruction. But like I said, you won't feel anything."

Feeling overwhelmed, she leaned her head back against the seat, took deep breaths, and tried to do exactly what Dawson had suggested--pray.

"Sheesh, you're not going to cry, are you?" Dawson asked with disgust. "I should have realized you'd be the emotional type. You're probably one of those who cries at sad commercials. Do you pass out when you're under stress as well?"

"No, I do not faint. And no, I am not crying." Rachel retorted, her voice tense with anger. Apparently, Rachel was right in her first impression of him. And, in her mind, he'd just ensured himself to be the lifetime recipient of the title, 'The Rudest Man.' "You assume these things about me when, the truth is, you know nothing about who I am."

"I know a lot more about you than you think. When you left La Guardia, we still didn't know for sure there was a bomb in your suitcase. But, given the fact that your suitcase just seemed to magically appear after being lost, I was fairly certain there was. We still had no idea what the intended target was, though, so we followed you. By the time we intercepted you at the hotel, you had been fully researched, and I knew more about you than I ever wanted to know."

The jerk! Rachel thought. Before Rachel could tell him exactly what she thought, Dawson began a recitation, as if he was reading from a file.

"Rachel Leigh Saunders. Born and raised in Justice, Montana, a small town about fifty miles outside of Helena. Uneventful life, good kid, no trouble with the law. Obtained a Bachelor of Arts in

Biology. Was registered for a Physician's Assistant program, but, when father had a heart attack, she decided to step into her father's shoes and run her family's ranch. Regarding a personal life, it does not appear as if she has one. No males have been linked to her name in any records, and, according to Facebook, she has never changed her status from 'single.' "

Rachel felt the anger and embarrassment staining her cheeks bright red. It seemed as if he had just mocked her entire life and threw her most personal struggles back in her face. It hurt to have Rachel Saunders reduced to the bare facts that in no way said who she really was.

"Let me repeat," Rachel said, her voice quiet yet tense with emotion. "You know nothing about who I am." Pausing, her voice brightened. "However, since you obviously know so many facts about me, I think it only fair to know one more fact about you."

Dawson's eyes narrowed in suspicion.

"You said your name was Dawson Tate. But, obviously that's a fake name--an alias, a stage name, whatever you want to call it. Great name for Hollywood, but in real life? Not so much. So, Mr. Hollywood, what's your real name?"

Rachel lips curved in a rather evil smile of satisfaction as she watched Dawson's sudden fury as he sputtered to find a response.

"Uh, Daws," Joe called from the front. "As much as I hate to interrupt the most entertaining conversation I've heard in weeks, we've got a problem. It looks like our friends are going to be insisting on that interview after all."

Both Dawson and Rachel turned around to see two dark sedans weaving through traffic behind the taxi, rapidly closing the gap between the vehicles.

"And the honeymoon is over," Dawson said. "They just figured out we know about the bomb. Joe, I hope you're current with your evasive driving training. We're going to have to lose them."

"Hang on," Joe replied.

Joe accelerated and began swerving around cars. After several sharp turns around corners, Rachel thought there were probably permanent imprints on the seat from her fingernails. It was just about as bad as the rides that spin at the fair, and Rachel already felt the carsickness coming in waves.

Dawson's phone beeped and he answered it, listening.

"You think?" He said, obviously angry. "We kind of already figured that out since we're currently being chased by the terrorists! You could have given us a warning that you were about to disable the tracking device."

Dawson was silent a moment. "You've got to be kidding," he finally said in disgust. "We can't hold them off indefinitely and, if you don't do something, you'll either have us dead and the bomb back in the hands of the terrorists or you'll have a bomb of unknown magnitude detonated in the middle of Manhattan! Since neither of those options are acceptable, figure this out NOW!"

Dawson pressed the button to end the call.

"What's going on?" Joe asked, his tone hesitant and suspicious.

Dawson punched the headrest in front of him in frustration. "I thought we had our best and brightest working on this thing, but instead it sounds like they've assigned the task to a room full of chimps. They hacked into the computer and were able to disable the tracking device, but not the bomb itself. They said they had intended to do both simultaneously, but only the tracking part worked. So now, the terrorists know we're on to them and might blow the bomb up at any time. "

"Okay, so where's the cavalry?" Joe asked, squealing the tires as he rounded a corner. "We need to take down these terrorists chasing us and get the bomb to a secure location, like five minutes ago."

"They aren't coming, at least not yet," Dawson replied. "The powers that be feel that if they show up in full force to take this thing down, the terrorists will detonate the bomb immediately. They are unwilling to risk it. Everything we know about this terrorist cell says they meticulously planned this and might be unwilling to forgo Plan A if it's still within reach. Bottom line, all enforcement has been ordered to stay away until the geeks can get this thing disarmed. We're on our own for now."

Joe let loose an impressive string of profanity. Followed by an immediate, "Sorry about that, Rachel."

"So they aren't going to help us all?" Rachel asked, her voice sounding small and frightened even to her own ears. Her eyes kept darting back to the bomb, expecting to see angry red numbers flash on the display at any second.

The two men didn't answer. All three were completely silent for the next few minutes as Joe drove like a maniac.

"Joe, you have to stay away from Midtown Manhattan," Dawson urged, apparently not liking Joe's choice of direction. "We're going to be too close to Times Square."

"It's not like I have a lot of choice here, Daws!" Joe replied rapidly spinning the steering wheel like it was the wheel of fortune. "They've tied my hands. I can't go near Times Square, the financial district, or any other major tourist destinations. Added to that, I can't go near any bridges or leave Manhattan. It's an island! And there are millions of people in the streets alone! Please tell me, where can I go?"

"You're right, Joe. Just do your best," Dawson answered.

Joe's best was pretty impressive. He must have been a star pupil in training for evasive driving. The scene out the front windshield looked almost like a video game; vehicles, people, and buildings going by in a blur. Rachel noticed, though, that he was trying to avoid the danger of traffic lights, choosing alleyways and side-streets with less congestion. Rachel periodically glanced to the rear and was amazed to see the two dark sedans keeping up despite Joe's talents.

"I'm not shaking them!" Joe finally admitted, his brow lined with sweat and frustration increasingly evident in his jerky movements.

"Joe, they've got guns!" Dawson yelled from where he was angled looking over the back seat.

"Get down and stay down, Rachel!" Dawson ordered, pushing her to the floor of the taxi. Putting the suitcase on the seat beside her, he further ordered, "Shut this."

As she hesitantly pushed the screen down into its original position and carefully zipped the suitcase back together, Dawson suddenly scrambled into the front seat while Joe was rounding a curve.

Rachel watched Dawson ready his gun and get into position, using the seat as a shield and cover.

Bullets hit the rear window, sending thousands of spider web cracks through the glass. Rachel ducked and covered her head.

"What are they doing?" She yelled to Dawson. "Aren't they afraid they'll hit the bomb?"

"It wouldn't cause any damage even if it did," Dawson replied. "The bomb is unbelievable in its technology. It would take an explosion to set it off accidentally. Otherwise, it will only go off if purposely programmed to.

Dawson peeked around the seat, but couldn't see through the rear window that was shattered yet still in place. Climbing back over Rachel, he leaned back and used his feet to repeatedly kick the window as hard as he could. It came apart in chunks that spun off behind them. Dawson scrambled back and took his position, now clearly able to see the enemy. Yet, he didn't fire his weapon.

"This is going to be tricky," he said. "I'm going to have to wait for the right shot. I don't want to encourage them to return fire. This area is too heavily populated. We can't risk any collateral damage."

It was driving Rachel crazy not to be able to see what was going on, but she was also too frightened to move a centimeter. So instead, she breathed deeply of the dirty carpet as she obediently lay plastered to the floor, eyes closed and praying for this nightmare to be over.

"Daws, this isn't working. I'm going to have to try something different."

Rachel felt Joe suddenly slam on the brakes, screeching the tires and fishtailing about 180 degrees. He then hit the accelerator and shot forward. Rachel heard a loud bang as something hit a window. The car immediately lost control. Panicked, she opened her eyes, sat up, and looked in between the front seats. Joe was slumped in the front seat with a gunshot wound to his head. He was dead.

Chapter 3

Before Rachel's mind could even process what was happening, she saw Dawson lunge at the steering wheel from his passenger's seat. Grabbing it with one hand and struggling to gain control of the wildly swerving car, he reached across Joe with the other hand, found the door handle, and opened it.

To, Rachel's shock, he unceremoniously pushed Joe's body out the car door and into the street.

"Dawson, no!" Rachel yelled, but it was too late. Joe was gone, and Dawson was now seated in the driver's seat. Quickly righting the car, the tires squealed as he accelerated and tried to design a maze which the other cars couldn't possibly follow.

"He was dead Rachel," Dawson said, answering her protest. "We will be too if I don't get us out of here. Joe can't help us now."

"But you just dumped him!" Rachel accused.

Dawson's phone beeped from where it had fallen on the passenger seat.

"Answer it, Rachel," Dawson ordered, focusing fully on the road as he sped down the street and marked the pavement with rubber tire tracks around every curve. Dawson was apparently equal to Joe in driving skills.

Reaching between the seats, Rachel got the phone and pressed the button to answer.

"This is Rachel Saunders," she said a little breathlessly. At the silence on the other end, she hurried to explain. "Dawson is currently… occupied, so he asked me to answer the phone." She stopped short of offering to take a message. That would just sound juvenile and stupid, even to her own ears.

"Tell Agent Tate we've already taken possession of Joe's body," a business-like voice said on the other end.

"They already have Joe!" Rachel reported. Dawson nodded as if he wasn't surprised.

"Also, let him know that we're tapped in to the grid now," the voice continued. "We're tracking his movements so he can go ahead and use the intersections with traffic lights."

"They say to tell you they're tapped into the grid, whatever that means," Rachel obediently reported.

"Good," Dawson replied. "That means they'll try to manage the traffic and turn the lights green for me to pass safely. Ask them how close they are to deactivation. I need help now!"

Rachel started to relay the question, then stopped. The line was dead. They had already disconnected the call.

"They already hung up."

"Figures," Dawson said. "We're still on our own."

"But now there are only two of us."

"So, you're going to have to help me," Dawson said. "I need you to get up here in the front seat, Rachel. You'll have to be the eyes in the back of my head. Do you think you can manage?

Rachel didn't reply. Instead, the second Dawson made a sharp right turn, she leapt into the front seat exactly as she had seen Dawson do earlier. Okay, so maybe not exactly. She probably wasn't quite as graceful, and Dawson may have gotten a foot in the shoulder. But she made it, and right before shots rang out once again from the rear. Apparently, her movements hadn't gone unnoticed.

Rachel struggled to fasten her seatbelt while Dawson swerved, trying to create a more difficult target. He veered to the right, then made a quick 90 degree turn into an alley on the left. A street vendor on the sidewalk in front of the alley, leapt out of the way in a blur of red, white, and blue.

The sky was getting dark in the gathering dusk, making details more difficult to see and the narrow alley seem more gloomy. The car barely fit in between the brick wall and the dumpsters lining the other side. Sinister shadows grew and seemed to take on a life of their own. Rachel wanted to close her eyes and wait for it all to be over, but she couldn't. It was like watching a train wreck, not wanting to see it yet unable to look away. She split her time between watching the swirling images in the front windshield and carefully peeking around the seat to the rear to see the lumbering, vicious shadow still pursuing them.

Dawson turned from the alley back onto a road. Still the sedan followed.

"Here we go," he said, the taxi fast approaching an intersection with a red light. It wasn't turning green. Cars were still passing through the middle yet Dawson wasn't slowing down.

"Dawson…" Rachel said hesitantly, not sure what he was doing. Maybe she had heard the man on the cell phone wrong. "Dawson…" this time more urgently. Maybe she had relayed the message wrong. The light wasn't changing! "Dawson!" she shrieked.

About two seconds before they entered the intersection, Rachel heard the sound of squealing tires as cars tried to stop suddenly. The light turned green, but there were still cars stuck in the intersection, misplaced due to the unexpected stop. Luckily Dawson was able to swerve through the gaps and make it across.

Watching through the now open rear window, Rachel thought the traffic light must have changed again right after they went through. Cars slowly began to move right when the dark sedan came through the intersection. The journey through 'the red sea' wasn't nearly as successful for those chasing them. The sickening sound of metal impacting metal made the rest of the world seem silent, yet the dark sedan made it across, having earned only a few ugly yet insignificant bodily injuries.

And still they kept coming. It was becoming increasingly clear that they were not going to be able to lose their stalkers. They were being hunted and the terrorists weren't about to give up and lose their prey, no matter what the cost. Rachel glanced over at Dawson, watching the muscles in his jaw twitch with the tension. He sat with his back straight but the lower half of his body slouched in the seat. At that angle, he was able to keep his head pressed firmly against the high headrest. Rachel realized these contortions were meant to keep his head out of sight so as not to provide a target for those following. Unfortunately, the awkward position looked very uncomfortable and made his evasive driving even more difficult. Dawson wasn't panicking, but Rachel recognized the subtle signs of stress and frustration. She knew he was fast running out of options.

"We're not shaking them, Dawson," Rachel said quietly. "How much longer can we keep this up?"

"I don't know," he replied, the stress making his words sound harsh. "Right now the only way I see for us to get out of this alive is if they get the bomb deactivated and a SWAT team of the A-team variety falls out of the sky. But, realistically, I'm thinking that even if they deactivate the bomb, no help is going to arrive soon enough to do us any good. What about you? Got any bright ideas, Montana? Maybe you wear a superhero costume under your other clothes just in case? I'm open to suggestions."

Rachel recognized that he was being facetious. He was about as open to her suggestions as he was to having a root canal without pain medication.

"Sorry, Hollywood," Rachel replied, matching Dawson's glib tone, "I only wear my superhero costume on Tuesdays."

But… maybe she did have an idea. A gun lay on the floor by her feet. She wasn't sure if it was Dawson's or Joe's. She also didn't know if Dawson was even aware of the gun and its location. Obviously, even if he'd had opportunity, he'd never be able to use it while driving.

Carefully, Rachel peered around the seat. The dark sedan had gained on them and was following only a short distance back. This would be difficult. She would have to time it just right.

Trying to be inconspicuous, she slowly reached down and gently lifted the gun off the floor. Dawson was so focused on driving, he didn't seem to notice her movements. Keeping the gun concealed against her right side, she pushed the release button on her seatbelt and waited.

"Dawson, they are pretty close behind us. If you let me know right before you make your next turn, I can try to get a good look at how many are in the car."

Dawson nodded.

About twenty seconds later, he announced, "Turning!"

In one smooth motion, Rachel swung her body around in the middle of the seats and raised the weapon. Taking a split second look, she confidently pulled the trigger.

The rearview mirror of the sedan shattered. As if in slow motion, thousands of glass shards caught the light from streetlights, flashing like miniature lightning strikes before inflicting horror on the car's inhabitants. Unable to complete the turn, the driver lost control, spinning out and hitting a street light before Rachel lost sight of it.

"That's a nice Glock. 40 caliber is my favorite," Rachel said evenly, replacing the gun on the floor and calmly refastening her seatbelt. "There were two, by the way."

Trying to keep his eyes on the road, Dawson still managed to gawk at her, the shocked and confused look on his face almost comical.

"Terrorists," Rachel explained, trying to clear his confusion. "There were two terrorists in the car."

"Who...? How...? How did you...?" Dawson stammered, finally finding his voice, sort of.

Rachel felt a thrill of satisfaction that she had managed to render the tough guy speechless for the second time that evening. "What?" She asked innocently, as if she had no idea what he was talking about.

"I didn't know you could shoot." Dawson said, finally gathering his wits enough to form a complete sentence.

"I'm from Montana. Of course I can shoot!"

"Why didn't you tell me what you were planning to do?" Dawson accused, his anger emerging as the shock began to fade.

"Would you have trusted me and let me do it if I had?"

"No," he admitted quietly.

"Besides, I wasn't sure I'd be able to take the shot."

"That was pretty impressive. How did you know you wouldn't miss and hit something or someone else."

Rachel shrugged. "My dad taught me to shoot when I was young. At the ranch, it's necessary to be a good shot in order to protect the livestock. But dad also taught me never to pull the trigger unless I was sure I could hit the target. I had a split second look at the sedan and the angle I needed. I knew I could make it. I wasn't aiming to kill. I knew the windshield wouldn't shatter, but the rearview mirror would. With the kind of damage the shattered glass would cause, there would be no way they could continue following. Trust me, it wasn't the most difficult shot I've ever made."

Dawson nodded as if he understood, but Rachel still saw a look of respect in his eyes that wasn't there previously.

"Next time, Montana, just tell me when you have a brilliant idea. Speaking of which, you took care of one, but what's your solution for getting us free from our other tagalong."

Rachel turned around and looked behind them. The last of twilight was quickly fading, which explained why Dawson was depending on her sight rather than his own rearview mirrors to spot a dark vehicle driving with its lights off.

"Uh… Dawson, what 'other tagalong'?" Rachel asked, seeing nothing behind them yet feeling a sudden sense of dread.

"The other dark sedan following us."

Rachel suddenly remembered that Joe had said there were two. She also recalled that when she initially moved to the front seat and started watching, there had been two cars in pursuit."

"Dawson, there was only one."

"Are you sure," he asked quietly, foreboding in his voice.

"Yes, I'm positive. I'm not sure when the other sedan dropped off but there has only been one following us for quite a while now. Now, there's no one."

In sheer frustration, Dawson hit the steering wheel with his hands.

"Rachel, get your head down now!" he ordered roughly.

Before Rachel could move, her peripheral vision caught sight of bright headlights out Dawson's window a fraction of a second before she felt the impact. She heard a scream of sheer terror, then realized it was her own.

Chapter 4

The car spun around and flipped. Rachel couldn't tell which end was up. In one sense, it felt like everything transpired so quickly, her brain couldn't process what had happened until after the fact. In another sense, it was as if everything was in slow motion. Every fear, every sensation seeming like it would never end. Would they never stop spinning?

"Rachel… Rachel, come on. We've got to get out of here."

She gradually became aware of Dawson pushing at her, trying to get her to move. The taxi had landed upside down. Before she could completely gather her wits, Dawson pushed her seatbelt release button and helped her maneuver into an upright position, which was very difficult with a deployed airbag in the way. Reaching across, Dawson found the door handle. As the door creaked open, Dawson began pushing her out of the car.

It was at that moment that Rachel realized his movements were hurried, frantic even. Her brain suddenly kicked into gear. She remembered what had happened and the danger they were in. Quickly, she untangled each of her limbs from the crumpled taxi and slid to the ground. Dawson must not have been able to get out his own door for, using her side instead, he slid to the ground beside her. But Dawson wasn't alone. Rachel's hated suitcase came out of the taxi with him.

Putting his finger to his lips, he motioned Rachel to be silent. Grabbing her hand with his free one, Dawson led her in crawling toward the front of the wrecked taxi. Once there, they discovered it had crashed into what looked like a large garage door. Where the front of the car had rammed into the door was a rather large opening.

They heard voices very close. Although they were speaking a language Rachel didn't know, she understood that they were inspecting the taxi, looking for them. Their absence from the vehicle was met with shouts of frustration.

More footsteps. Were those getting closer?

"Go, Rachel! Go!" Dawson whispered, urging Rachel to crawl through the hole in the door.

Their movements failed to go undetected. Rachel heard an excited shout, then rushing feet. Out of the corner of her eye, she saw Dawson draw his weapon and fire, trying to buy them some time. As answering gunfire hit the building, he scrambled through the opening after Rachel. She heard their enemies clambering behind them even as she and Dawson struggled to their feet and began racing through what appeared to be a warehouse.

Their own footsteps echoed staccato on the concrete floor, providing an audible trail for those chasing. As if realizing this, Dawson suddenly grabbed Rachel and pulled her behind some kind of large wall or partition. Pressing into the deepest, darkest corner, they waited. The interior of the warehouse was pitch black. Trying to assess her surroundings, Rachel could only make out shapes in varying shades of black.

Although their own steps were now silent, the warehouse echoed the rhythm of what sounded like many other footsteps, all looking for them. Rachel thought there was probably only four of them, but the echoing effect of the warehouse multiplied their steps in every direction. To Rachel there seemed to be an ominous rhythm to the sound, like what she would imagine African drums would sound like when beating a funeral dirge.

One set of footsteps stood out from the others. It was close. Too close. Dawson stood in front of her, putting his arms around her, and pressing her back close to the wall. Rachel tried to shrink as far back as she could, willing their shapes to blend in with the darkness and go unnoticed.

A flashlight beam skimmed within inches of their position. Rachel's breath caught, then accelerated. Her body shuddered with gasps, yet she couldn't seem to get enough air. Still the footsteps kept coming. So close now! They were going to be caught!

Dawson suddenly shifted position, reaching one hand up to cup her face. Then his lips were on hers. Shocked, Rachel tried to turn her face away, but he held her securely, his silent lips gentle yet insistent. Why was he kissing her? Maybe he knew they were going to be caught. Maybe he wanted to share this one last moment before they would surely be killed--a glimpse of what might have been.

He caressed her cheek with his fingers as they slowly trailed up to catch in her hair. Succumbing to his kiss, Rachel put her arms around his neck and returned his every emotion. The kiss was slow and almost achingly tender. His lips moved across hers in a way that made her feel loved and cherished, yet still very much desired. The gentleness couldn't mask the passion that lay under the surface.

Yet, it wasn't a happy kiss, full of promise and dreams of the future. Instead, it was as if it was forbidden and this was the only time he would ever be allowed this indiscretion. Rachel's fear and surroundings faded away. The only thing that existed for her was Dawson. For that single moment, as he held her close, Rachel felt his every emotion, his vulnerability. And then, it was as if he slammed the door. When Rachel felt she could go on kissing him forever, Dawson suddenly stopped, pulled completely away, and removed her arms from around his neck.

Rachel fell back to reality hard, frantically straining her eyes and ears to figure out what was happening. Flashlight beams bounced off every wall as if performing a choreographed light show. Footsteps still echoed, but they were all distant now.

Dawson grabbed her hand once more and quietly led her toward some dark shapes lined up against a wall. With each step, they softly planted a foot before putting any weight down, trying to be as soundless as possible. Dawson stopped as one of the flashlight beams came within a few feet of them then moved on.

Finally reaching the dark shapes, Rachel saw that they were actually large crates. Gently, Dawson removed one of the lids and peered inside. Replacing it, he went to the next one.

Apparently, finding this one acceptable, he motioned for Rachel to climb inside. Dawson crawled in after her, bringing the suitcase with him and lifting the lid back in place over top of them. The crate was large, but space was still tight with its new occupants. Rachel had never been claustrophobic, but sitting in a completely dark, cramped crate with a bomb while terrorists searched for them was enough to make her start reconsidering her position on the subject.

Taking out his phone, Dawson pushed a button and waited.

"We're trapped," he whispered, apparently confident his soft but urgent words would not reach outside the box. "We need extraction, now!"

In the close silence of the crate, Rachel could easily hear the other side of the conversation as well.

"We can't do that, Tate. We don't have the bomb deactivated."

Rachel felt Dawson's whole body tense with anger, but he only whispered, "How long?"

"Not sure. We are making progress, but this is technology we've never seen before."

"What are we supposed to do? They wrecked the taxi, we're sitting in a crate in a warehouse while they search every inch of the place."

"You've got to sit tight, Tate. Stay hidden. Maybe they won't find you. If they do, you are authorized to use whatever force necessary to keep them from taking possession of the bomb. We're working as fast as we can. You're one of the best we have, Tate, but we can't risk more agents, let alone civilian lives if we were to try for an extraction and have the bomb go off. As long as the terrorists think you're alone and the bomb is still recoverable, we don't believe they'll detonate it."

"So, for all intent and purposes, I am on my own."

The voice on the other end was silent. Then, "I'll let you know the second it's deactivated."

The call disconnected. Rachel felt Dawson lean his head against the back of the crate.

"So, I guess we just...?" Rachel whispered softly.

"Wait," Dawson replied. "Wait for the terrorists to find us or for my buddies to get the bomb under control."

Rachel felt wave after wave of helplessness. She could only imagine what Dawson was feeling.

Dawson sat for several minutes in silence, leaning his head back. If the quarters and position had been slightly less miserable, Rachel would've thought he was relaxing.

Seeming to finally remember her presence, Dawson lifted his head and asked quietly. "Are you hurt? You probably have a concussion. I think you got knocked out. Do you have any other injuries?"

At first, Rachel had no idea what he was talking about. Then the memory of riding in the taxi, being hit, and crashing rushed over her. Escaping and surviving since then had been such a top priority, she had blocked the crash out. For the first time, she took inventory of herself. Body parts all accounted for? Blood? Pain?

"I think I'm okay," she finally answered, matching Dawson's whispered tone. "I have a headache and probably some nasty bruises, but nothing major. And you?"

"I'm fine. A gash on my arm, probably some bruises, nothing major. The airbags all deployed. I told you to get your head down because I thought they'd try to shoot at us from the side. I didn't anticipate them hitting our car with theirs."

"Why would they bother shooting us when they could just crash our car and knock us into a building? What is this place anyway? It's some kind of warehouse, right?

"We're in the part of Midtown Manhattan called 'Hell's Kitchen.' It used to have many warehouses, but most of them are long gone or have been converted to other buildings. I didn't get a good look at things outside, but I think this bottom level is still a warehouse while the upper levels have been converted to offices. By the products inside the other crate, I'm guessing it might be a distribution warehouse for some of the cruise ships that dock in the Manhattan area. The corporate offices are probably upstairs. I guess it doesn't really matter what it is though. The building is empty of everyone but us and the terrorists trying to kill us."

Both Rachel and Dawson fell quiet. For Rachel the hopelessness of the situation felt close and suffocating. Of course, the fact that they were in a small confined space probably intensified those feelings. There didn't seem to be a way out. The terrorists would either find them and kill them to get the bomb, or, if finding them was too much trouble, they could just detonate it and have the same result-- their death.

As they sat in the ominous silence, Rachel gradually became aware of just how physically close Dawson was to her. The tight space required her to be snuggled up against him. There was no part of her right side that wasn't touching his left. Suddenly, the air inside the crate seemed tense and heavy with sudden awareness and attraction. Rachel wanted to ask Dawson about his kiss, but she felt too awkward. Turning toward him, she tried to peer through the dark to read his face. He had to be feeling this same magnetism. If she could just see or touch his face, maybe she could read him and know.

She felt a touch on her cheek and leaned in to Dawson's caress.

As the physical pull became almost unbearable in its intensity, Rachel choked out, "Dawson...?"

Dawson jerked his hand away, startling like he'd just had a bucket of ice water dumped on him. The spell was broken.

"Did you grab Joe's gun off the floor of the cab?" He asked, his tone all business

Rachel's mind spun, trying to catch up to Dawson's abrupt question. "No, it didn't occur to me at the time. I didn't even know it was Joe's gun. I'm sorry."

"Can't do anything about it now," he said, shifting and reaching his hands up to the lid. We'll just have to make do without it."

Without pausing, he continued, "I'm going to open the lid a little since we haven't heard any action in quite a while. No more talking. No noise at all, you got it?"

Irked at being treated like a child, Rachel still managed to nod her head. Then she realized, with satisfaction, that Dawson probably wouldn't even be able to see her nod.

Regardless, Dawson moved the top of the crate off a little and waited. There was no sound. There almost seemed to be an eerie hush over the whole building. Not a single footstep, not a voice, not even the groans or creaks of an old building.

After several minutes, Rachel did notice something. At first she dismissed it. She must be imagining things. Then it became stronger. Finally, she could deny it no more. Breaking Dawson's order for silence, she whispered, "Dawson, do you smell that?"

Dawson, as if just waking up, immediately began scrambling to get his feet under him as he said the one word Rachel was dreading to hear.

"Fire!"

Chapter 5

Shoving the lid off completely, Dawson bolted upright out of the crate, the danger of terrorists fading significantly with the immediate threat of fire. Standing up beside him, Rachel's eyes immediately began burning. There were no flames yet visible, but the warehouse was rapidly filling with dense smoke that, if possible, made Rachel even more blind in the dark interior. Feeling an immediate shot of panic, her hands frantically fumbled for Dawson. Connecting with his arm, she grabbed it with both her hands, afraid that if she let go for a second, she wouldn't be able to find him.

Rachel heard Dawson search for his phone with his other hand, then heard the beep of him sending a call.

"They set the warehouse on fire!" he practically yelled into the phone. "I need satellite images and building specs RIGHT NOW!"

After listening for about ten seconds, he continued. "We don't have a few minutes! I need to know how to get out of here now! In a few minutes we'll be dead!"

Rachel started coughing. She couldn't seem to get the smoke out of her lungs.

"Do it!" Dawson replied, disconnecting the call.

"Get down, Rachel," he said, pulling her down to the floor beside him. "We have to stay low where the smoke isn't so bad."

"What did they say?" Rachel choked out, her throat feeling like sandpaper. "Did they tell you a way out?"

"They're working on it, but we can't wait. We're going to have to start crawling to the nearest exit."

"And how do we know where that is?"

Dawson's phone beeped. He looked at it. "They sent me some of the building specs as well as our location in the building based on my tracking beacon. The wall directly north of us is an exterior wall with a door. Let's head there."

"But which way is north? We'll probably end up wandering around in circles!"

"Thank God for apps," Dawson said, his cheerful tone contrasting sharply with their situation. "I just so happen to have a handy-dandy compass and flashlight on my phone."

They crawled as quickly as possible across the cement floor on their hands and knees. Rachel focused on breathing and maintaining physical contact with Dawson at all times. She found if she breathed through her nose rather than her mouth, the air seemed to burn a little less.

Dawson pushed the suitcase ahead of them, rolling it along on its wheels. Knowing he couldn't push the suitcase, crawl, and drag her with him at the same time, she had to settle for making sure her right shoulder kept constant contact with Dawson's body.

They never made it to the wall. Instead, they located the source of the smoke. Bright flames danced in their path.

Dawson yanked out his phone.

"They started fire around the entire perimeter of the building! We can't get out!" Although he was yelling to be heard over the snapping fire, his voice was raspy from the smoke. Pausing, he listened. "You have the satellite feed?" Listening again for about ten seconds, he then started yelling. "That's not good enough! Get us out of here!"

When the call ended, he reported to Rachel, "The satellite feed shows every exit is covered by waiting terrorists. We can't get out."

"Are they sending people to come get us?" Rachel rasped, panic threatening to overwhelm her.

"No. Our lives aren't worth the others that could be potentially lost. They're supposedly trying to come up with a plan, but we don't have time."

The flames were getting rapidly closer. Heavy smoke was filling the warehouse like it was a glass bottle. Even with her face pressed to the cement floor, Rachel felt like she couldn't breathe. Fireworks started exploding in her vision. She knew she didn't have long.

"Dawson... I... I..." she couldn't finish her sentence. She couldn't even remember what she'd wanted to say in the first place.

"Hang on, Rachel! I'm not going to sit around waiting for us to die." Reaching out, he grabbed her arm, dragging her, trying to get her moving. "Rachel, come on! I have an idea. Get moving!"

Struggling to maintain consciousness, she roused herself enough to follow Dawson a few yards toward the middle of the room where the flames hadn't reached. Through the flickering light, Rachel could see a large machine, probably like a forklift. Although Rachel was not an expert on warehouse machinery, she thought it was probably used to move heavy equipment and objects, like the crate they had hidden in.

Climbing up into the machine, Dawson started the engine. As she watched him, Rachel pulled her shirt over her mouth and nose, desperately trying to filter out the smoke and keep alert. Coming back down to her, Dawson explained his plan.

"I'm going to set the machine to drive forward. Hopefully, it'll hit the large warehouse door and keep going. We have to follow behind it so that when the terrorists are distracted by it, we can escape."

Rachel was still aware enough to feel paralyzing fear. "But the flames! We'll have to run through the flames?"

"There's a clear path to the door Rachel! We can make it! They probably purposely lit the whole perimeter, except the exits on fire, leaving us a way to come to them. Come on, Rachel! This is our only chance!

Not waiting for her response, Dawson pulled her to her feet and placed one of her hands on the back of the machine. Taking her other hand, he wrapped her fingers around the handle of the suitcase.

"You're going to have to take it, Rachel. I have to drive the forklift and jump off right before it crashes. You can do this."

Rachel found herself nodding, but it was almost an out-of-body experience. She felt numb, as if her body was on autopilot while her mind was strangely disconnected.

Coughing heavily, Dawson managed to climb up to the forklift once again. As it began moving forward, Rachel's feet moved as well, keeping time as it rapidly increased speed. Before her mind could catch up with what was going on, Rachel found herself running in between the flames.

Nightmares of being caught in a burning building couldn't compare with the reality. She could feel the intense heat, burning through her clothes to her skin. She imagined the flames grabbing, reaching for her as she passed. She gasped for air, but it was so hot and laced with smoke so acrid that it smoldered all the way down. Fire burning from the outside, and fire reaching down her throat, burning from within.

The forklift was going too fast now. She couldn't keep up, losing her handhold on it. But still she ran. Amidst the roar of the fire, she heard a loud crash. The forklift in front of her faltered but kept moving. She heard men's voices yelling as she tripped over rubble and flames still licking at her heels.

Emerging into a blackness that seemed less dense, Rachel tried to suck in great mouthfuls of air, but her lungs were so filled with smoke, she just coughed all the more.

Suddenly she felt someone grab her arm and pull her rapidly to the right, away from the forklift, away from the building. She had no strength to protest, but stumbled as the insistent hold on her arm pulled her along. In the distance she could hear the sirens of fire engines.

After what seemed like a long time faltering on unsteady legs through alleys and around buildings, the person leading her pushed her up against a wall in a dark alley and held her there.

"Rachel, are you okay?" Dawson's voice! Raspy and barely above a whisper, but definitely Dawson! She sagged with relief and exhaustion. Dawson caught her, supporting her weight and holding her close.

Rachel tried to speak, but no sound came out. Instead, her efforts triggered another bad coughing spell. Dawson helped her slowly sit on the cold concrete. Walking a few steps to the corner, Dawson peered around.

Turning back to Rachel, he said, "Don't move, Rachel. I'll be right back."

Rachel didn't think she could move even if she wanted to, but Dawson was back in less than a minute, unscrewing the cap off one of two large bottles of water and handing it to her. Rachel drank eagerly, feeling the cool water all the way down to her stomach.

"Thank you," Rachel whispered, sound finally croaking past her swollen throat.

Dawson nodded, sitting down next to her in the alley. Sitting on the concrete with their backs up against the brick wall of a building wasn't the most comfortable position, but, at the moment, Rachel was too exhausted to move.

Dawson spoke. "We should probably both be treated at a hospital for smoke inhalation, but that's not really possible at the moment. We'll just have to do the best we can."

"Have you talked to your superiors? Do they know we got out of the warehouse? What are we supposed to do now?" Rachel asked, her mind finally kicking into gear and spinning with questions. Unfortunately, her voice wasn't quite recovered enough to keep up and about every other word was missing in her speech.

"They already know we got out," Dawson said, apparently able to fill in the blanks and understand. "They're tracking me, remember? They'll call me if they have any news. Until then, I don't really feel the need to report our every move. It's not like they were much help when we were trapped in the fire. And, they certainly didn't do anything to help prevent Joe's death. It's obvious that, to them, we're expendable. No, I think we're better off on our own, at least until they actually come up with a plan."

Beneath the anger, Rachel also recognized feelings of helplessness and grief.

"My head was down in the taxi, and I didn't see what exactly happened to Joe," she said. "But, short of sending in the A-team, I doubt that there was anything anyone, including you, could have done to prevent his death."

"They should have sent someone," Dawson muttered angrily. "We couldn't lose them. Joe got desperate. He slammed on the brakes and spun around, trying to catch the terrorist off guard and head in the opposite direction. As he hit the gas and passed them, one of them got a good shot in at our side. Joe was killed instantly. If we'd had any kind of help, Joe wouldn't have even tried to pull a stunt like that in the first place."

Rachel reached out and gently took Dawson's hand in both of hers, trying to offer comfort

"I'm so sorry, Dawson," she whispered, rubbing his calloused hand lightly with her thumb. "I know Joe was your friend. It had to be very difficult to lose him like that.

"It's not the first time I've lost a friend."

"I guess that doesn't make it any easier," Rachel said. "Had you and Joe been close friends for long?"

Dawson shifted, trying to find a more comfortable position. Looking at her, he said abruptly, "Your face is filthy."

Okay, so Rachel could take a hint. He did not want to talk about Joe. Still reeling with the jolt of shock and embarrassment from his unexpected words, she rummaged around, trying to find something, anything, to clean her face off.

"Here, I'll do it," he said, his voice surprisingly kind. Pouring some water from the bottle onto the sleeve of his jacket, he used it to gently wipe Rachel's face, his motions soothing and almost tender as they caressed her skin. She closed her eyes as he touched her cheeks, her eyes, her neck. Rachel felt the air around them become charged once again with an awareness of each other, an undeniable attraction and connection that she couldn't ever remember feeling with another man.

As his hand finally slipped from her face, Rachel opened her eyes, her gaze locking with his in the dim glow from a nearby streetlight. Pouring some water onto her own sleeve, she returned the favor, carefully wiping the dark soot and dirt from the masculine planes of his face. But, instead of closing his eyes with her ministrations, Dawson's dark blue gaze remained on her unwavering, making her slightly self-conscious with its intensity.

Finishing, Rachel's hand dropped. Dawson blinked, breaking eye contact and restlessly shifting his position. The moment was over and was quickly replaced by the cold dampness and lurking fear of the alley.

As the minutes passed, Rachel found herself fidgeting with her hands, becoming increasingly uncomfortable with the tension from Dawson's silence.

"Rachel," he said finally, "we've had to be very close for the past few hours, much closer than usual for two people who have just met. I know I've even had to kiss you twice in order to keep you safe. But, you need to know, I don't plan on making a habit of that. I don't want you to get the wrong impression."

He paused, as if trying to choose just the right words. Then, giving up, he blurted, "I have no interest in you romantically."

Chapter 6

Rachel felt humiliation wash over her in waves. Had she really been that wrong in reading him? Had she really been that obvious in her interest? She had been so sure of their mutual attraction. Now, to find out she had been completely wrong was like someone had just pulled a chair out from under her right as she was going to sit down.

Rachel was a confident young woman in every area of her life, except one. Now, all of her insecurities about her love-life came flooding over her. He didn't want her. He didn't like her. There must be something wrong with her that no decent guy ever seemed to be interested in her romantically.

"Can I ask you a question?" Rachel asked calmly. "You said you had to kiss me twice in order to protect me. How exactly were you protecting me when you kissed me in the warehouse?"

"You were breathing too heavily," he answered simply, unemotionally. "One of the terrorists was getting too close. You were so scared you were practically hyperventilating. Your breathing was loud and irregular. I knew he would find us if he heard you, so I did the only thing I could think of to get you quiet fast."

"You kissed me because I was breathing too heavily?" Rachel asked, disbelief in her tone.

"It's not like I could have verbally told you to be quiet. Kissing you was the fastest way to shut you up."

"But did you have to do it so thoroughly?" Rachel demanded, her anger rising so rapidly that the normal filter from her brain to her mouth wasn't working properly. From previous experience, Rachel knew this greatly increased the chances of her saying things she would later regret.

"Look, I'm sorry if you felt misled. I was just doing my job, and right now, you and your protection are part of that job. It's really nothing against you personally. I make it a policy to never get involved with women from the cases I work. Ever."

"I understand," Rachel said, her serene voice contradicting her true emotions. She stood to her feet.

"And if it makes you feel better, I really don't think you misled me. In your mind, you were just doing your job."

"Yes, I was," Dawson said, also rising and standing beside her. "I'm glad you understand."

Rachel took her half empty water bottle and removed the cap, as if to drink. Suddenly, she jerked the bottle forward, flinging a heavy stream of water straight into Dawson's face and chest.

"Oh, I'm sorry!" Rachel crooned, feeling intense satisfaction at watching Dawson sputter. "I don't normally do that kind of thing. I actually make it a policy to never fling water at unsuspecting men. Ever. But, I guess sometimes someone who really deserves it comes along, and, I don't know what comes over me. I have to make an exception. But, don't worry, Hollywood, I don't plan on making a habit of it."

As Dawson ran his hand down his wet face, Rachel thought she detected a glint of humor in his eye, but she couldn't be sure.

"Come along, Montana, we need to get moving," he said, obviously choosing a timely retreat from their previous discussion. "I heard sirens headed toward the fire. Our friendly terrorists are going to know that we escaped from the building, and they're not going to want to stick around after the fire department sets up camp."

Dawson once again took possession of the suitcase as he and Rachel began walking to the other end of the alley.

"I don't even understand why they set that fire in the first place," Rachel said, more than willing to call a truce, at least for now. "Weren't they afraid that the fire would ignite the explosives in the bomb?"

"No. I think the metal case that houses the explosives is probably fire proof. Worst case scenario would be that the fire would destroy some of the wiring. But that would be easy to replace, and the important part of the bomb would still be intact. Ideally, I think they were hoping we would try to make an escape out of the building and bring the bomb to them."

"But what if we didn't? Why would they risk it? They wouldn't be able to retrieve the bomb with the building in flames and the fire departments arriving on scene."

"Don't underestimate these people, Rachel. They're professional terrorists and have spent much of their lives planning for situations like these. More than likely, they were ready with some uniforms that would enable them to blend in with the firemen until the fire was out. Then, they could just go in and retrieve the bomb."

Rachel thought, still not completely satisfied with the explanation. "But how would they know where to find it? That warehouse had a lot of square footage. How could they even hope to locate a suitcase in it, especially after it had been heavily damaged by fire?"

Having reached the end of the alley where it met the street, Dawson suddenly stopped walking, a strange look on his face. "They would have had to… track it!"

Dawson grabbed Rachel's shoulder and pulled her into the shadows. Clutching his cell phone, he made a call.

"Is tracking on the bomb still disabled?" he asked urgently. "Are you sure? Check again."

Rachel gradually became aware of footsteps approaching slowly from at least two different directions.

"Never mind," he snapped.

Hanging up, he caught Rachel's hand in his free one and whispered, "Keep close."

They turned and ran down the sidewalk. Although Dawson tried to keep to the shadows, the streetlights stationed at regular intervals were still able to illuminate their progress. The sound of running footsteps echoed from behind them.

Rachel had no idea what Dawson's plan was, or even if he had one. But, they were already both tired and winded from the fire. There was no way they could outrun the terrorists, and there was no way they could sneak through the shadows and escape. Even if they could manage to lose their pursuers, it wouldn't be for long if they were being tracked as Dawson suspected. It seemed hopeless.

But, surely, they wouldn't shoot them in the back here on the street. There were too many cars, and the sidewalks were increasingly filled with people. Nevertheless, Rachel braced herself, waiting to feel a gunshot hit her back even as they dodged around other pedestrians.

Though Rachel's lungs felt like they would burst, they hadn't run far before Dawson took a sharp left, leading her to a building with a long line of people out front. Going directly to the front of the line, Dawson showed some kind of card or ID, and the sentinels moved aside to let them in.

As they walked through the door, Dawson leaned over to Rachel's ear. "If they really are tracking us, then our best chance is to be around lots of people. We won't be open targets, and, hopefully, it'll be much more difficult to pinpoint our exact location."

Rachel looked around the large room, finding that they were in a crowded nightclub. A long bar ran along one side while most of the open area was taken up by a sea of dancing people. At the front of the room, a live band was playing deafening music while overhead, multicolored lights blinked and partied to the beat.

Holding her elbow, Dawson guided Rachel through the room, passing sights that were so foreign to the Montana girl they may as well have been visiting another planet. People, many of them wearing very little, were dancing in contortions that Rachel had not ever imagined. The fluctuating lights in the dark room gave everything an eerie, unreal look. Reaching the very center of the room, Dawson stopped. Still holding the suitcase in one hand, he grabbed Rachel around the waist and began dancing.

Dawson must have seen the stark terror in her eyes and misinterpreted it. "Relax. Just dance like everyone else and maybe they won't even notice us."

"I can't," Rachel said, shaking her head adamantly. "I have no idea how to dance like this. I can do a pretty good line dance, and my brother taught me how to swing, but this…? No."

Dawson actually laughed at her fear, pulling her closer. "Don't worry. You gave a great performance in front of your hotel earlier. Just do it again. I can handle having my toes stepped on for one night. It's not like I'm going to make a habit out of dancing with you."

Rachel glared at Dawson, feeling her earlier anger replace her fear, which, she later realized, was probably exactly what Dawson intended.

Leaning in closer to him, she began swaying to the music, mimicking some of the movements of the people around her. Warming up, she threw herself into the role. Gyrating, messing with her hair, leaning in toward Dawson--she figured if she was going to do it, she might as well go all the way and look absolutely ridiculous like everyone else.

Dawson's nearness sent goose bumps creeping along her skin. Feeling the pressure of his body next to hers as they danced made her pulse race. Rachel once again felt the current between them, like the attraction between two magnets. *Stop, Rachel,* she ordered herself firmly, closing her eyes briefly and trying to talk the feelings away. *It's not real. You're nothing to him. It's all in your imagination.*

She avoided his eyes, imagining his scorn and knowing he'd be able to read the emotions on her face. She needed a distraction.

Purposely pressing close to him, she spoke into his ear. "You stink, Hollywood… literally."

"Trust me, Montana, you don't smell like a rose either."

Rachel realized, after being in a fire, they probably looked about as good as they smelled. Dawson's clothes were filthy and the smell of smoke was overpowering. Of course, she would have to claim at least half of that odor as her own. She was somewhat amazed that their appearance didn't seem to be attracting the attention of those around them. But, given the smorgasbord of fashion already on display, maybe that wasn't so surprising.

"Time to start making our exit," Dawson said abruptly, still dancing but pulling Rachel along to the opposite side of the room from where they entered.

Looking over his shoulder, Rachel saw at least two men threading their way through the dancers and zeroing in on their location. She lost sight of them as

Dawson moved more rapidly through the club. Using a door behind the stage, they found themselves in a storage area obviously meant for employee use only.

Before they made it to the door marked 'Exit,' they heard the other door they'd just come through slam shut. Quickly, they pushed open the large metal exit door and entered the alley that ran behind the building. To the right was a dead end. The wall of another brick building cut off any escape that direction. To the left, the alley extended the length of the nightclub before meeting with another alley running perpendicular.

"They're too close behind us," Dawson said hurriedly. "We'll never make it out of here, especially with them tracking our every move."

He took out his gun and positioned himself behind the door. "We're going to have to make our stand here. Get behind the dumpster, Rachel," Dawson ordered, indicating the large metal dumpster in the corner.

Heart pounding, Rachel obeyed, crouching on the other side of the dumpster, but making sure she still had a good vantage point for watching Dawson. They waited.

Suddenly, a gloved hand clamped over Rachel's mouth and she was pulled back roughly. A muscular forearm held her back tight against her assailant's body. She couldn't move. She couldn't scream. She felt the pressure of something cold and hard on her temple. Though completely dark, it took less than a second for Rachel to realize she now had a gun to her head.

Chapter 7

Dragging her from behind, her assailant pulled her back toward Dawson. As her feet tripped and slid across the pavement, Dawson whirled their direction right as the door to the nightclub opened. Another terrorist stepped out, immediately aiming his gun at Dawson.

"Put down your gun nice and slow," the man holding Rachel said calmly, his voice free of any identifiable accent. "If you try anything, she's dead."

Dawson immediately put his hands up in surrender, his gun still in his right hand. Slowly, deliberately, he began to put it down, making every effort to show his cooperation.

Rachel's thoughts went on overdrive. She knew the second Dawson's gun hit the ground, they'd both be killed. Guns were trained on both of them. There didn't seem to be any scenario where they would live past the next few minutes.

She couldn't let Dawson put that gun down. Even if she was killed, Dawson had to stay alive so he could prevent the terrorists from getting that bomb. If she was going to die anyway, she might as well make it count. Her daddy didn't raise a girl who would go down without a fight.

Within the split second it took for the flood of thoughts to rush through her head, Rachel reacted. She quickly turned her head to the left, directly toward the barrel of the gun. The movement loosened her attacker's grip on her just a fraction. Immediately her right hand shot up, grabbing his gun hand. Spinning out of his hold, her left hand grabbed the gun and twisted it backward out of the man's hand. Before the terrorist had even realized what she was doing, Rachel had escaped and now held his own weapon trained directly to his forehead.

Rachel heard a gunshot. Keeping her eyes on the shocked terrorist in front of her, she shifted her position to see Dawson standing upright, gun into firing position. Apparently, with his gun almost to the ground, he had seen Rachel's movement, brought his weapon up and fired at the terrorist whose gun was aimed at him.

Confirming his enemy on the ground was dead, Dawson confiscated the dead man's weapon and came over to Rachel. Removing a pair of handcuffs from somewhere, Dawson handcuffed the other terrorist.

Rachel heard a sound, like a small piece of metal rolling across the asphalt.

"Come on," Dawson said quietly. "We have to get out of here."

They sprinted back to the door of the nightclub, Rachel grabbing the suitcase while Dawson brought the prisoner.

Backs against the wall, Dawson paused, as if indecisive which direction posed the least risk.

"I saw at least two terrorists following us in the nightclub," Rachel whispered.

"This other one was obviously waiting out here to cover this exit," Dawson mused. "One came out the door, but where is the other one from inside?"

Gunshots rang out, hitting the walls and pinging against the metal dumpster.

"I guess that answers that," Dawson said, pulling open the door and reentering the building.

Pulling the large metal door shut behind them, he locked it and slid several other deadbolts in place. He then looked around the darkened back stage area.

Opening a door to his left, he pulled their prisoner in behind him and motioned for Rachel to follow as well. While the terrorist wasn't putting up a fight, he also wasn't accommodating. He moved slowly, as if waiting for a rescue or an opportunity to escape. His limited cooperation was probably only obtained because Rachel still kept the weapon steadily pointed at its owner.

The room they entered was more like a large closet, obviously used for storage and maintenance supplies. An exposed light bulb hung from the ceiling, providing an artificial glow over the heavily-stocked shelves and the equipment and other junk stationed in the corners and randomly throughout the room.

Wasting no time, Dawson patted down the terrorist, searching him from head to toe. He found no other weapon but removed his wallet and some other small items, which he stuffed into the front pocket of the suitcase.

Grabbing a white barkeeper's apron off a shelf, Dawson gagged the prisoner. Rummaging around, he located some long cords like those used to tie back curtains. Quickly, Dawson expertly tied the man's hands and feet.

Dawson's phone beeped. He answered it and listened.

"Thank God!" He breathed, then reported hurriedly. "We apprehended one of the terrorists. There are others around, so we have to get out of here now. You'll have to come pick him up. He's gagged and tied up in the storage closet backstage. Just look at my tracker right now and mark the location."

He paused and listened. "How close...? Okay, got it."

After hanging up, he bent to check the ties one more time to make sure the prisoner was secure.

Rachel asked, "If you were going to have your associates pick him up, why did you take his wallet?"

"A little insurance," Dawson replied. "I don't have time to question him. There's always a chance he will escape, be killed, or kill himself before they can collect and question him. If that happens or if he just refuses to talk, at least we will have some info and a lead to track down."

Returning to the door, Dawson shut off the light and cautiously opened the door a crack. Seeing and hearing nothing, he opened it wider and stepped back into the backstage area. After Rachel followed, Dawson shut the door behind them, leaving the prisoner in the dark. They retraced their steps from earlier, going back to the entrance of the nightclub.

"They said the tracking device on the bomb has been disabled again," Dawson whispered. "But, we still have to make it out of here. Our best chance is to go back through the nightclub and try to blend in with the crowd."

As Dawson's hand turned the knob, Rachel suddenly realized she still held a gun in her hand. Dawson had a holster of some kind that hid his gun beneath his jacket. Rachel had nothing. Not knowing what else to do, she impulsively lifted the bottom hem of her shirt and placed the gun underneath it. Thankfully, the gun was very small, but it was a little unnerving to feel the cold weapon against her bare skin.

As they reentered the nightclub, she kept her hand on the gun from outside her shirt and tried to make her hand position cover the shape of the gun and look as natural as possible. Hopefully, her shirt was blousy enough that the casual observer wouldn't even notice.

Dawson didn't bother dancing and playing the part this time. Instead, he made a beeline for the entrance, heading straight through the middle of the dance floor and swerving around the closely packed couples. Rachel had difficulty following his erratic path.

They reached the entrance right as a large crowd was exiting. Grabbing Rachel's free hand, he positioned them in the center of the throng as they moved outside. Their connected hands kept them from being separated by the jostling bodies around them.

Once outside, the tightly packed crowd loosened. Keeping their hands together, they walked quickly with the pedestrian traffic for several blocks. At a busy intersection, Dawson finally paused. Rachel realized this intersection must have a lot of nightlife destinations, as there was heavy traffic on both the streets and sidewalks.

"This seems like a good place to be inconspicuous for a few minutes," Dawson said, backing them up into the shadows of a building.

They stood in silence a few moments as Dawson seemed to focus on analyzing every detail of their surroundings.

Finally, he gently pulled Rachel to stand directly in front of him.

Placing his hands on her shoulders and looking directly at her, his gaze intense, he said, "First, you used a gun better than most professionals, making an unbelievable shot to take out the car chasing us. Then, you escaped from a terrorist with a gun to your head, disarmed him, and took him prisoner with his own weapon!" With shock and admiration in his eyes, he asked in a completely awed and bewildered voice, "Who ARE you?"

Rachel had an insane desire to giggle. "You read my file--my dossier. Remember?" she replied. "You already know everything there is to know about me. I'm nobody special. Just Rachel Saunders from Montana."

Now that they were finally standing still, the effects of the adrenaline were catching up with Rachel. She was breathless, and her legs felt weak and wobbly. She suddenly realized her hand was cramping as it still had a death-grip hold on the gun under her shirt. Taking the gun out, she handed the weapon to Dawson with shaky fingers.

"You keep it," he said, refusing to take it. "Obviously, you need and deserve your own gun."

"I already have plenty of my own guns. I just couldn't bring them on the plane," she said, trying to keep her tone of voice steady.

Rachel looked down at the gun in her hand. Dawson wanted her to keep it, but it made her nervous. She didn't know what to do with it. But, she also realized that for safety, she probably needed to keep it in case something happened and Dawson needed help. Finally, lacking a better place, she returned it back under her shirt. Thankfully, the Walther 9mm was so small it was easy and inconspicuous to carry. She'd recognized it as one of the newer weapons, one she probably would have loved to take target practicing under normal circumstances. But, now, it had lost a little of its appeal.

She felt Dawson's eyes on her, but ignored him, focusing instead on masking her shaking limbs. She needed to seem strong and capable, but her body was playing the traitor. Now that she was just earning some respect from Dawson, she didn't want him thinking she was a weak, dependent female.

A couple seated on a bench a few yards to their left got up, leaving the bench vacant. To Rachel's relief, Dawson moved to sit down. Her legs felt like wet noodles, and she hadn't been sure how long they could keep supporting her. Reaching the bench, Rachel's muscles felt like they finally gave up the ghost and she plopped down. Dawson sat uncomfortably close. Rachel had to stop herself from scooting further away to recover her personal space.

"So, Rachel Saunders from Montana, how did you learn to shoot like a sniper and fight like a black belt?"

"My dad," Rachel replied. "He has a black belt in karate and is also a very good shot with almost any kind of gun."

"Sounds like a guy I'd like to know." Dawson's voice was casual and matched his relaxed position as he lounged on the bench. Yet, though seemingly unperturbed, Rachel noted there was still tension in his body and his eyes never stopped moving as they scanned every detail of their surroundings.

Trying to mimic Dawson's laid-back attitude, Rachel spoke. "My older brother, Phillip, has never really shared any of the same interests as Dad. Even as a kid, he never liked the ranch and had no desire for Dad to teach him anything. So, my dad taught me. I had to learn to shoot to protect the animals at the ranch. Dad always said I was a natural shot. He also wanted me to learn to protect myself. He taught me everything, including how to disarm an opponent who had a gun to your head--not that I've ever had to use martial arts in a real life situation before. I'm happy to know that it actually works."

"And it apparently works very well," Dawson said. "What about your brother? Did your dad end up eventually teaching him too?"

"No, Phillip has made his own path just about as far away from Montana as he can get. He's currently in Florida and loving it. He and my parents are still on great terms. They've always allowed him the freedom to follow his own dreams and make his own choices. But, I'm probably a lot closer to our parents than he is, simply because I love the ranch and share their interests."

With a jolt, Rachel felt Dawson's arm move across the back of the bench and pull her close. She shot a glare his direction.

"What?" he whispered innocently yet with a wicked gleam in his eye, as if he knew exactly what he was doing and was thoroughly enjoying her discomfort. "We have to keep up appearances."

Rachel responded with a seething stare, but didn't move away.

"Your dad must be very proud of you," Dawson said conversationally, continuing their previous topic as if nothing had changed.

After being so ornery, was he now trying to flatter his way back into her good graces?

"You were obviously a great student for him," he continued.

Rachel shrugged, trying to get over her discomfort. "I guess I've always been a Daddy's girl."

"It's a little more than that, Rachel. I mean, you were quite impressive. I didn't think we were going to make it out of that alley alive. I had no idea you knew how to do something like that, let alone that you would be courageous enough to try it. You had a gun to your head! I don't think most agents or law enforcement officers could have done what you did." Dawson's restless eyes settled on her thoughtfully. "Maybe I should say YOU ARE quite impressive."

Rachel ducked her head as she felt her face warming from his praise. She certainly didn't feel like she deserved it. She had never felt fear like she had when that gun was to her head. But, she had known that their only chance to survive was for her to do something. So, she did what her dad had trained her over and over to do. Brave? No. Courageous? No. Desperate and scared past logical reason? Definitely yes.

Rachel finally risked a glance up at Dawson and couldn't look away. His intense eyes locked with hers. She felt the web of attraction drawing them together.

In the dim glow from the streetlights, Rachel saw his eyes darken. He was so close now.

"Dawson," she breathed softly. "If you kiss me again, I'll save the terrorists the trouble and kill you myself."

Dawson's eyes flew wide with shock, severing their connection and ending the intimate moment.

"I'm sorry for being so blunt, Dawson," Rachel continued, making her voice sound sweet and genuinely contrite. "But, I'm only telling you this for your own protection."

Dawson's blue eyes lit with humor. He threw his head back and laughed. But before he could collect himself enough to speak, his phone beeped.

His laughter stopped abruptly, a serious mask replacing the gorgeous smile, dimples, and sparkling eyes.

"Tell me what you have," Dawson said into the phone, not bothering with any formalities.

Dawson listened for about thirty seconds.

"Okay, got it. We'll be there." He disconnected the call.

"What's going on?" Rachel asked anxiously.

"We have a plan," Dawson reported. "They've figured out early on that the bomb uses a cell phone detonation. They located the phone number and were able to hack in and disable the tracking initially. Unfortunately, the terrorists are doing their best to maintain control, and our resident hackers are still having trouble with the encryption for the detonator. They say they're very close though, and, once they get it, the bomb won't be able to be activated remotely. It will be safe to be transported to a secure location where it can be completely disassembled."

"So, what's the plan? Are they going to come get us?"

"No. As I said, they're close, but they haven't deactivated it yet. We have to buy a little more time and get in position. We're supposed to make our way down to the dock." Dawson gestured back the way they'd come from the nightclub. "It's not very far-- within walking distance. Hopefully, we'll time it right so that, when the bomb is neutralized, we'll be met by other agents there at the dock. They'll take possession of the bomb and transport it out of Manhattan."

Dawson stood from the bench, as if ready to get going immediately.

"But how are we going to get from here to the dock?" Rachel asked, feeling a fresh wave of fear wash over her. "If we go that direction, we'll have to pass by the nightclub again. The terrorists are still going to be looking for us."

"Come on," Dawson said, not answering her question. Instead, he gently grasped her elbow and propelled her along beside him as he walked rapidly through the shadows, retracing their steps back the way they had come. They hadn't walked far before Dawson stopped in front of a door.

He turned to Rachel, saying, "They will be looking for people who LOOK like us, but they won't be looking for us."

A bell over the door jingled as Dawson pulled it open. Rachel followed him inside and looked around, trying to figure out where they were and what they were doing here. Dawson wasted no time in moving around the shop, quickly grabbing merchandise seemingly at random.

Rachel felt her eyes grow wide and her mouth gape open. She had never been in a shop like this before. After shuffling through terms from her somewhat limited, sheltered Montana experience, she finally mentally categorized it as an 'adult novelty shop.'

Coming to her senses, Rachel stopped gawking and took off after Dawson.

"Dawson…? Dawson!" She followed on his heels, urgently trying to get his attention, to ask him why they were here. What could he possibly need right now from a shop like this?

She felt her face blushing. Being in a shop like this made her feel very naive and embarrassed. Part of her didn't want to look around, inspect, or even know what 'novelties' the shop boasted. But, despite the strong urge to put her hands over her eyes, she also had an insane curiosity. She was observant enough to realize the shop's merchandise wasn't all of the 'adult' variety. Souvenirs, apparel, and other items catering to tourists were also displayed.

Finally, Dawson turned to Rachel and pushed a large pile of clothes and other items into her arms.

"There's a changing room back there," he said, pointing to the rear of the store. "Go change into these clothes."

The item on the top of the pile was a red wig.

A disguise! Everything suddenly clicked together and made sense. That's how they were going to get to the dock without being recognized.

Dawson didn't wait for Rachel's response, but immediately set off searching for what Rachel assumed would be his own disguise.

She obediently found the little closet they called the fitting room and drew the curtain behind her. It would be so nice to have clothes on that didn't reek of smoke! She only wished she could also get a shower!

She quickly removed her smoke saturated shirt and pulled on the shirt Dawson had given her.

That was strange. It was a classic white 'I Love New York' shirt, but Dawson must have grabbed the wrong size. It was really short and tight, hitting her mid-torso.

Wondering if Dawson's other picks were equally small, she looked through the rest of the pile.

Skirt: short, black, tiny. Though slender, Rachel was tall. She wasn't sure that skirt would fully cover her rear-end.

Black fishnet stockings. Did anyone nowadays wear those things outside of a Broadway musical?

Black boots: ridiculously high-heeled and tall. They looked like the tops would extend at least to her knees.

And, of course, the wig: bright red with long, wavy tresses.

As she shook out the wig, a makeup kit fell to the floor. The colors were very bold and bright. Normally, she would never willingly use these colors unless she had to dress as a clown for a little kid's birthday.

With everything spread on the floor around her, the light bulb went off in her head, and she realized what it all meant. Shock was quickly followed by red hot anger. Dawson expected her to dress as a hooker.

Chapter 8

After sitting on the floor of the fitting room and fuming for several minutes, Rachel's reason prevailed. She jerked on the offensive clothes and slathered on the makeup. As much as she would like to, she couldn't even give Dawson a much deserved tongue-lashing right now. The top priority was getting to the dock safely so they could get the bomb out of their possession and off the island of Manhattan. If she had to dress like a hooker to get that done, she would sacrifice her pride and do it with gusto. She wasn't going to waste precious time arguing with Dawson over his taste in disguises. She may not have a choice at the moment, but that in no way meant the man would escape completely unscathed. She would just have to postpone his punishment.

Clothes on, makeup applied, Rachel finally turned to the wig. Her own blond hair now hung in tangles and mats instead of its usual waves. Gathering it together and fastening it with a few pins included with the wig, she then secured the red mane.

Her ensemble complete, Rachel looked at herself in the mirror and grimaced. Her makeup was heavy, but not grotesque. The bright red lipstick made her pale skin appear almost porcelain, and the red wig stood out like fire. The tight clothes hugged her body, accentuating her long legs and curvy figure.

Rachel felt very self-conscious, especially about her bare abdomen. She wasn't used to exposing her belly button for all to see. She was about as far out of her comfort zone as she could get. Despite her insecurities, Rachel had to admit that, to the casual observer, she probably made a great-looking hooker. Almost too good. Dang that Dawson Tate!

Turning back to gather her stinky clothes, Rachel saw the gun lying on the floor. What was she supposed to do with that? Dawson had insisted she keep it, but it wasn't as if she could hide it under her shirt anymore. Her current disguise allowed no spare inch to hide anything on her person, much less a gun. Turning around the little room, she spotted a black purse on the floor. Dawson must have included it with the other things. She just hadn't noticed it before now. It was small, but the 9mm fit inside perfectly. If she didn't know better, she might accuse Dawson of being very thorough and almost thoughtful. But she definitely knew better. The jerk!

Rachel shoved aside the curtain and stepped out of the changing room.

Dawson was waiting. His eyes flew wide as he very conspicuously looked her over from top to bottom.

"Wow!" he said. "You look…"

"I didn't realize this was your type, Dawson," Rachel interrupted.

"It normally isn't. But, Montana, you are hot!

"I'd take that as a compliment if I wasn't currently dressed as a prostitute!" Rachel pinned him with an accusing glare.

Dawson grinned. "I wasn't even sure you'd put the clothes on."

"I didn't think I had a choice," Rachel replied. "Don't worry, though. I fully intend to get back at you for making me wear this."

"Hey, you're not alone here, I'm not exactly dressed as a missionary either."

"No, you aren't. I think my cornea has been damaged from just trying to look at you in that suit."

Saying the suit was brightly colored was an understatement. Its brilliant lime green color was so intense, it seemed to exude its own glow. As if the suit wasn't bad enough, his head was topped with a matching lime green hat. Rachel had no idea why such an atrocious suit would even be manufactured let alone why someone would buy it, even as a disguise. She understood that she was dressed as a hooker, but what exactly was Dawson supposed to be? Then it suddenly hit her.

"Are you... Are you my pimp?"

Dawson's teeth flashed white in a grin. "Rachel, it's only pretend."

"You are!" Rachel's whisper was still a shriek. "Dawson this is ridiculous!

Dawson shrugged, ignoring her ire. "Come on, let's get going. You'll have to leave your old clothes here. We can't carry them. I've already paid for everything else."

Knowing she needed to put aside her fury at least for now, Rachel dutifully stuck her clothes in the black garbage sack Dawson handed her. She couldn't say she was heartbroken about forever abandoning her smoke damaged clothes.

Sticking the sack behind the counter, Dawson started for the door, pulling the ever-present suitcase behind him.

"Wait, Dawson!" Rachel said, putting her hand on his elbow to stop him. The clerk was across the shop not even looking their direction, but she lowered her voice to a whisper anyway. "That suitcase is a dead giveaway. Even with the best disguises, they'll know it's us as soon as they see that suitcase."

"Lots of people carry suitcases like this around," he objected.

Rachel raised her eyebrows.

"Fine," Dawson said, grabbing a can off a nearby shelf.

Before Rachel could say a word, he was spraying haphazard lines of neon blue paint all over the suitcase.

"There," Dawson said, finishing and placing the can back on the shelf. "Now maybe it won't be quite as recognizable."

"That's my suitcase! Rachel protested in shock.

"No, it's not," Dawson retorted, his intense whisper not reaching beyond Rachel's ears. "This suitcase and its contents are now the property of the U.S. government."

Rachel opened her mouth to argue, but let it snap shut instead. She had nothing to say. Realistically, after everything that had happened, she wouldn't want it back even if she was given the chance.

Leaning past Dawson, Rachel reached for the can of paint. She aimed at the suitcase and sprayed a few more of the neon streaks into the material, completing their modern art masterpiece.

"There, that's better," she said, tossing the empty can into a nearby trash bin.

"Alright then," Dawson said. Turning back to the clerk, he waved and called across the shop, "Sorry about the smell!"

"Hey, no problem," the clerk replied cheerfully.

Rachel didn't know how much Dawson had paid. The tags on her new clothes and accessories had never been scanned or even glanced at by the clerk. But, judging by the happy smile from the satisfied clerk, the payment had been enough to cover their disguises, the can of paint, and the unpleasant aroma of said spray paint used indoors.

Once outdoors, Dawson put one arm around Rachel and pulled her close. "Okay, Rachel, now you have to play the part. Stick close. We've got to take this a little slow. We don't want to attract any attention by trying to set a speed record."

They set off sauntering westward down the street with Rachel obediently staying nestled under his arm.

"How are we supposed to be inconspicuous when we're dressed like this? Rachel grumbled.

"Sometimes the best way to hide is to be the most visible," Dawson responded. "They certainly aren't going to be looking for two people dressed as we are. They'll be watching for a couple trying to keep to the shadows and blend into the crowd. We are way too flashy and obvious. They won't even take the time to consider us. Besides, in this part of town and at this time of night, we'll fit right in."

Rachel was still doubtful, her anger still seething under the surface. It must have shown.

"Come on, Rachel. It's not like I did this on purpose. I didn't have a choice either. I had to work with what we had on hand. We're almost done with this. You can have the rest of your New York vacation and then head back to home-sweet-home. You can manage to be uncomfortable and dressed like a knock-out hooker for a few blocks until we get rid of this thing. This will work. I know it will. Trust me."

Rachel blew out all the air in her lungs with one big whoosh. "Okay," she relented.

"Good girl. Now we need just one more Oscar-worthy performance, Montana. Pull on your best hooker persona and act like you like me--a lot."

Rachel obediently wrapped her arms around him as they walked.

Every once in a while she'd stand on her tiptoes, press herself close to his side, and whispered sultrily in his ear things like, "You're still a jerk," and, "I'm going to get you back for this."

His eyes were constantly moving, watching for signs of danger, but, for the most part, Dawson played his part cool and in control. She was his possession.

At one point, though, after one of her whispered endearments, he grabbed her close and whispered back. "Careful, Montana, or I just might decide to take the risk and kiss that orneriness right out of you."

She was just choosing what whispered sweet-nothings to challenge him with, when she felt a hand grab her right arm and pull her roughly out of Dawson's hold.

She was suddenly face to face with a large man with bad body odor and equally stinky breath. The light from the streetlights showed him to be fortyish with the face of a thug, but he was surprisingly well-dressed in a polo shirt. Unfortunately, he smelled as if he had already ingested at least one bar's entire stock of whiskey.

"How much for this pretty woman?" he asked, running his rough finger down Rachel's cheek.

Before he even finished his sentence, Rachel was jerked roughly out of the thug's hold and back into Dawson's arms.

"Sorry, dude," Dawson said calmly. "This one isn't available. Tonight she's mine."

"Come on, man," the thug replied. "Have a little love. I won't take her long. There's a place I know right around the corner. Then you can have her back. Just tell me how much."

Two other men behind the thug, apparently his friends, made similar comments showing their support of his plea.

"Sorry," Dawson reiterated. "The answer is no."

Still holding Rachel possessively, Dawson turned to continue on their way.

The man grabbed Dawson's arm, obviously becoming increasingly agitated and angry. "Come on, dude. Let the whore do her job."

Unbuttoning his suit jacket, Dawson replied, his voice deadly calm, "I think you and your friends better move on and find some other entertainment tonight." Slowly, he moved his jacket aside to reveal the gun at his waist.

Instantly, having a change of heart, the man put up his hands and backed away, saying, "Hey, sure, man, I didn't mean anything."

Grumbling, his friends followed suit, backing away before turning to leave.

Rachel hadn't realized how scared she had been until the man left. Then she fell limp against Dawson's side. Supporting her weight, Dawson turned and continued walking west toward the dock.

Rachel was still trying to find her voice to thank Dawson, when he spoke first, "Now I know you could have taken care of those thugs yourself, Montana, but thanks for letting me handle it. It helps a guy's ego if he gets to come to a lady's rescue every once in a while.

"Thank you, Dawson," Rachel said seriously.

"Stay close." he said. "We may not be out of the woods yet. You make way too hot of a prostitute."

Rachel tried to resume her play-acting, but it was difficult. Her senses were on high alert now for two kinds of enemies. Her eyes darted to and fro, searching for both terrorists and men who might be appreciating her a little too much. She had no idea what either of the enemies should look like, but that didn't stop the adrenaline from pouring through her and putting her body on high alert.

At one point, Dawson stopped, backed up against the wall of a building, and pulled her against him. Though he gave no word of explanation and didn't attempt to kiss her, to a passing observer, it would appear as if they were sharing an intimate moment. Rachel was facing Dawson with her back to the street and passing people, but she watched as Dawson's eyes seemed to be following someone. Finally satisfied that the danger had passed, Dawson stepped away from the building and pulled Rachel back down the sidewalk.

Dawson had been right about them blending in even with their outrageous disguises. It seemed like, in at least this part of town, any attire was acceptable. There were fashion examples on every end of the spectrum, many get-ups bordering on the ridiculous. And the people were as diverse as the fashion. There were hookers, street performers workers, partiers, gang members, men in business suits, and even a preacher. The hour had to be getting late, and yet the sidewalks were packed. There was no sign that the nightlife was going to be winding down anytime soon either.

For the most part, Dawson and Rachel went unnoticed. The only attention they got was from prostitutes who hated Rachel on sight, sending evil glares her direction, and from men whose eyes raked over her hungrily. She felt like a high quality cut of steak. A few times, Rachel saw men plot intercept courses, but Dawson shook his head, giving them a negative answer before they even asked. With his fierce look and possessive stance, they seemed to get the message and tried to pass it off as if they had never intended on making a proposition in the first place.

Rachel saw a strip of space devoid of lights up ahead. Assuming that the black abyss was water, Rachel realized they must finally be getting close to the dock. Dawson had said it wasn't far, but, whether due to danger and fear more than actual time, this walk had certainly seemed endless. But while she was wanting to pick up the pace now that their destination was in sight, Dawson seemed to hang back, his steps slowing.

"Is this the dock where we're supposed to meet?" Rachel asked impatiently. "What's wrong? What are we waiting for?

There was a large cement area that led down to the water. Yet Dawson was fully stopped now, carefully scanning the entire area and looking confused.

"Something isn't right," he mumbled, lost in his own thoughts.

"What? What isn't right?"

"We shouldn't be here."

"What are you talking about, Dawson? This was the plan."

"Yes, but why are we here? If the tracking signal wasn't working and the terrorists had no idea where the bomb was, why didn't they detonate it? We should be dead."

With a feeling of dread, Rachel understood Dawson's point. "Maybe…" but she couldn't think of any reason why they wouldn't set off the bomb if it had completely lost their control. It would be more dangerous for them to have it fall into other hands that could use it to identify them and their methods.

Rachel saw a man walking toward them from further down the dock. Dawson must have recognized him because he didn't seem alarmed.

"Tate, glad you made it," the man said, shaking Dawson's hand. "I'm Paul Simmons. We have everything ready. I just got the call that they've successfully deactivated the bomb. Everything should be good to stick it in the helicopter and get it out of here. We've got two other agents down there to ensure the area stays secure. One of them is the helicopter pilot. He and I will be taking possession of the suitcase and flying it to its next destination. A team of other agents will be here in a few minutes to escort you and Miss Saunders to safety."

As if he hadn't heard a word Paul Simmons had said, Dawson turned to Rachel. "Unless…" he said, continuing the previous topic. "Unless they never fully lost control of the bomb. Unless they knew they would be able to find it again."

The world was completely silent for the space of two heartbeats.

"Rachel, get down!" Dawson's yell came a split second before he body-slammed her into the ground.

Everything exploded in gunfire.

Chapter 9

Rachel couldn't breathe. Hitting the ground had completely knocked the air out of her lungs. Dawson fell on top of her. As the gunshots beat a staccato rhythm through the air, he crouched over her, shielding her with his own body. The second there was a break in the barrage, Dawson scrambled off and literally dragged Rachel behind some large crates.

"Rachel, are you okay," he asked urgently as his hands checked her for any injuries.

Rachel still couldn't speak, but managed to nod.

Simmons had managed to scramble to safety nearby as well. Both he and Dawson took out their phones.

"We have shots fired!" Dawson said into the phone. "They knew where to find us. Is the tracking device still disabled? Check it!"

More shots were fired. Dawson peeked around the crate, watched a few seconds, and then returned fire.

"Great! Why weren't they already in position? It'll be too late by the time they get here. They're already closing in on our position."

Dawson soon disconnected the call and turned to Simmons. "Tracking is enabled again."

"How is that possible?" he asked. "We had it disabled."

"I don't know. Maybe the tech guys were so focused on deactivating the bomb that they didn't notice the terrorists working to reactivate tracking."

"So what do we do?" Rachel asked, finally finding her voice.

While still peeking around the crate and trying to determine the enemy's position, Dawson answered, "The bomb is still deactivated, so they are sending a team of agents now to assist us in apprehending the terrorists. The problem is that we're a good ten minutes from having those reinforcements."

"Ten minutes!" Simmons fumed, his hands fumbling as he reloaded his gun. "We'll be dead by then! Why didn't they have a team ready?"

"They said they didn't anticipate this problem and were trying to keep very few agents involved until the situation, meaning the bomb, was fully under control. Obviously, we can't wait that long. I'm sure they've identified our position and are working even now to surround us. We have to get to the helicopter and get this bomb out of here. They suggested that, if we could have the bomb in position by the helicopter when the rest of the team arrives, they will be able to cover the departure and apprehend the terrorists so they can't track it."

"There's one problem with that," said the other agent. "I just spoke on my phone to the two agents trapped down closer to the helicopter. The pilot was hit in the first attack. He'll live, but there's no way he can fly."

"I'm trained to fly a helicopter," Dawson said. "I guess I'll have to do it."

Of course he's a helicopter pilot, Rachel thought irritably. Was there anything the man couldn't do?

"We have no idea how many of them there are, but we can't stay here," Simmons said. "I'll follow and cover you the best I can. What about the girl?"

"She's with me," Dawson answered.

"Okay, let's do it."

Dawson turned to Rachel. "Are you up for this?"

"I'll be fine," she replied, trying not to think about bullets zinging past her head.

"Follow me. You'll have to stay close, but keep low."

There were crates and machinery littered around the dock. They methodically ran with their bodies hunched from one shelter to the other, pausing, watching, listening, and then running again. Rachel heard gunshots following their movements. Heart pounding, she fully expected to feel the bullets ripping into her, but either the terrorists were bad shots or their movements too furtive for them to be accurate. Dawson didn't return fire, probably not wanting to give away their exact location. Simmons held his fire as well, simply following and trying to safeguard the immediate vicinity.

Rachel could see the outline of the helicopter. They were close. Suddenly a gunshot sounded at close range. Rachel tucked her head down as several more ripped through the air, all close but from slightly different locations. Rachel realized the truth. The terrorists had been guarding the helicopter, knowing it was their original plan of escape. Now that they had tried to approach it, she realized they were probably surrounded. They had walked into a trap.

Simmons was a few yards behind her, on the ground, returning fire. Dawson crouched behind a large crate a few yards in front of her. Although his weapon was drawn, he didn't return fire. Rachel realized he wouldn't want to risk giving up their location unless it was absolutely necessary.

The dock was illuminated by a bright overhead street light, but Rachel still couldn't see anything clearly outside of about a twenty foot radius. She knew Dawson was still trying to conjure up a way to make it to the helicopter, but Rachel couldn't see how it would be possible to get there with both the suitcase and their lives. Although not constant, gunfire was coming from at least three different directions. They couldn't go forward and they couldn't move back. They were trapped.

The gunfire seemed to die down, at least for the moment. Rachel lifted her head in time to see a shadow disengage from the rest of the darkness and sneak up on Dawson's side.

Dawson must have caught the movement out of the corner of his eye. He swung around and raised his gun, pointing it at the man's chest. At the same time, the attacker raised his weapon, pointing it directly at Dawson's chest. They were in a deadlock. Guns pointed at each other. Neither willing to give up.

"Drop your weapon and hand over the suitcase," the shadow said clearly.

"No thanks. I don't think I like that idea," Dawson said.

Dawson was going to be killed! Rachel knew that even if he handed over the suitcase, he'd still be shot. She had to do something. Carefully, so as not to attract attention, Rachel began to move forward, closer to Dawson as the men talked.

Rachel noticed that this man, like the other terrorists from the alley, had no accent. Why would terrorists trying to detonate a bomb on U.S. soil sound American?

Rachel had now maneuvered herself into a position where she could see the attacker more clearly. While she still couldn't see his features, she got a good look at his gun arm fully extended from his body. Silently, she opened her purse and pulled out the 9mm Dawson had insisted she keep.

"I guess I could just kill you and then take it," the man said.

"No, that's not going to work," Dawson replied. "You might kill me, but you won't touch the suitcase. You'll be dead."

Rachel was aware that the circle was getting tighter as the man's associates were slowly closing in on Dawson's position as well. Simmons was rapidly firing his gun, already engaged in his own fierce battle.

Lord help me! Rachel breathed as she brought the gun into position and held it steady. *Careful, Rachel, careful,* she coached herself. *You can do this.*

"That's not necessarily a bad deal," the terrorist mused. "My colleagues will collect the suitcase. Such a sacrifice would be honorable for a man like me. What about you? Are you ready to die?"

"You first."

Rachel pulled the trigger. The terrorist screamed, the shot almost knocking him over as he dropped his weapon and grabbed his injured hand. She'd hit her target.

Other shadows began converging on Dawson. He jumped back behind the crate and began firing.

"Rachel, the suitcase!"

Rachel hurriedly shoved the gun back in her purse, then drew the strap over her head and one arm so it hung diagonally across her body. Wasting no time, she shot to her feet and sprinted for Dawson. Trying not to think about the shadows turning their attention to her, she grabbed the suitcase with both hands, lifted it off the ground, and raced for the helicopter.

The stupid wig was loose and kept getting in her eyes, making it difficult to see. Catching movement out of the corner of her right eye, Rachel ripped off the wig with one hand, turned toward the oncoming attacker, and threw the hairy beast in his face. She didn't wait to see if he stopped, and she didn't even register the pain of ripping the wig with its attached pins off her head. She had to make it to that helicopter.

Finally, reaching the passenger's side door, she searched for the handle. *How the heck do you open a helicopter door?*

Someone grabbed her shoulder. Wheeling around quickly, she broke the hold, knocking the assailant's hand away with her forearm. Catching the gleam of a gun in his other hand, she reacted instinctively. She blocked the gun with her left forearm at the same time as she brought her left leg up in a front kick directly to the man's groin. Before he even had a chance to react, she then shifted her weight and used the same leg to land a hard side kick with the heel of her boot directly in his gut.

Her movements were seamless, the entire sequence lasting no longer than a second. Moaning, her attacker fell to the ground. Right now, survival was paramount in Rachel's mind, to the exclusion of her usual thought patterns. Normally, Rachel hated the thought of having caused someone pain. But her dad had trained her that when facing a real attacker, never pull any punches (or kicks for that matter).

Once again, she jerked at the helicopter door, finally pulling it back. She hefted the suitcase up, climbed in behind it, and shut the door. It was a small helicopter. Her feet were practically on the seat to make room for the suitcase on the floor. Seconds later, the door opposite her opened. Dawson climbed in, his movements almost frantic.

"The cavalry is here, but we're not safe yet," he announced as he quickly pulled on a headset and began pushing buttons. "They'll have a good battle that I'm not planning on sticking around for."

Rachel could hear rapid gunfire outside, but it didn't seem directed at the helicopter. That was probably deliberate since it would be too dangerous to risk igniting an explosion with the bomb inside. The case might be able to withstand some fire, but Rachel doubted it could withstand being engulfed in an exploding helicopter.

Dawson handed Rachel the other headset and started the helicopter. Her stomach flipped as it left the ground. Dawson quickly gained altitude and headed south over the Hudson River.

Dawson pushed a button and said, "We have cleared the dock and are currently traveling southward. I need to know our destination."

Rachel could hear Dawson clearly through the headphones and could also hear the response on the other end.

Directions and coordinates were rattled off to Dawson. They made no sense to Rachel, but Dawson seemed to understand.

"The tracking signal has also been disabled again," the voice on the other end added. "With both it and the remote detonation deactivated, you shouldn't encounter any more trouble. Agents are rounding up the terrorists at the dock, and we'll have a team waiting to take possession of the bomb at the facility."

"Roger that," Dawson replied, ending the transmission.

As they reached the bay, Rachel could see the Statue of Liberty in the distance. She was glued to the window as the helicopter passed close. Had this weekend gone according to plan, she would have been seeing it under vastly different circumstances. To be sure, this helicopter flight was definitely thrilling, just not for any reason she'd ever expected.

Leaving the Statue of Liberty behind, Dawson continued south over the bay. At his current speed, Rachel couldn't imagine it taking them terribly long to reach their destination, wherever that may be.

Having a sudden thought, Rachel lifted the suitcase onto her lap and began opening it.

"What are you doing?" Dawson asked.

"I was going to remove my clothing from the suitcase. It doesn't really have anything to do with the bomb, and I'd rather not have a bunch of scientists sifting through my underwear. Is that okay?"

"I guess," Dawson replied, his tone showing a little uncertainty.

Rachel reached into the suitcase and removed her nightgown, shirts, and panties that were on top of the bomb and to the side. She had no idea what had happened to the rest of the contents of her suitcase.

She unceremoniously balled the clothing together and placed it at her feet.

She began to re-zip the top of the suitcase. Something flickered on the bomb's display screen. Angry red numbers appeared on the screen, then rapidly changed, counting down. Rachel watched in horror. 2:00... 01:59... 01:58... 01:57...

The bomb had been activated.

Chapter 10

"Dawson!" Rachel managed to squeak out.

Glancing over at Rachel, he saw the changing display. His startled eyes shot to Rachel, the fear and helplessness written there conveying much more than words could express.

Breaking contact, his hand slammed the radio button.

"The bomb is active!" he yelled into the headset.

"That's impossible!" said the voice on the other end.

"I don't care if you think it's impossible! The numbers on the display say otherwise. This thing is going to blow in less than two minutes! 1:40... 39... 38..."

"Okay, okay!" the man conceded. We have no way of deactivating it." There was a pause. Then, "I'm sorry, Tate... you're going to have to get that thing as far away from Manhattan as you can in the time you have left."

"That's it, then?" Dawson asked. "Just, 'Sorry you're going to die. Do your best to minimize other collateral damage?'"

"I'm sorry, Tate," the voice replied with regret. "We're out of options. There's nothing we can do."

"Well, that's not good enough." Dawson ended the transmission.

1:20. Dawson already had the helicopter going wide open, flying at a dizzying speed while also increasing his altitude. Rachel looked down below, watching the land on either side of the bay come together, then separate wide as they entered the larger, lower bay.

Dawson spoke rapidly, "Okay, Rachel, I figure we have one shot at this." Rachel had to concentrate to keep up with Dawson's hurried words. "We have no idea how strong this bomb is, so I'm trying to get as far away from the city as possible. We'll have to push the suitcase out of the helicopter, but we have to time it just right so it explodes above the surface of the water. If we time it wrong, then the bomb will explode underwater, possibly causing a massive concussion wave that could hit the shore and cause serious damage. If it explodes too close to the helicopter, we'll be dead. The other option is to take my superior's advice and just go down with the ship."

"Let's go with option number one. What do I need to do?"

"I have to fly the helicopter, so I can't be the one to push the bomb out."

"I'll do it."

40 seconds.

"Push it out with about 20 seconds left. I'll hold it steady so hopefully we won't create a vacuum when you open the door.

Rachel put one hand on the door handle and the other hand on the suitcase, watching the numbers on the display count down.

25… 24…23… Rachel pulled the handle and swung the door outward. She hefted the suitcase toward the open door. It wasn't moving. She pulled and pulled. It wouldn't budge.

"It's stuck!" she yelled, fear and frustration consuming her voice.

The wind from the open door whipped her hair around her face, making it difficult to see. Hands shaking, she reached below the suitcase and pulled up from the bottom. The corner moved. Jiggling and pulling, she inched the suitcase out.

Her frantic eyes caught the red display. 16...15...

With all her might she threw the suitcase at the door, the effort making her lose her balance and launching her body toward the opening.

Down, down the suitcase fell.

Rachel tried to grab something, anything to right herself. Her hands caught the extended handle on the door. Off-balance, she shifted her weight, trying to get the door closed. The instant Rachel pulled the door into place, Dawson took off, trying to give them more distance from the explosion. He'd said they needed 20 seconds. She hadn't given him that.

Unfortunately, Rachel hadn't gotten her door completely shut. It was in the correct position, yet she couldn't get it latched. She struggled with the handle, but the door wasn't fitting securely against the frame and wouldn't lock in place.

"Dawson... Dawson, my door!" Rachel called, panicking and trying to get his attention. As if still watching the display, her mind had continued the countdown, fully expecting her life to end. 3... 2... 1...

Nothing.

Then, suddenly, the helicopter was hit. She saw nothing, and yet it felt like a giant hand knocked the helicopter down like a toy. With the first jolt, Rachel's door was wrenched open. She was flung from her seat directly into the open door. Her fingers, still holding the door handle, locked in a death grip halting her fall.

Dawson struggled to maintain control as the helicopter twisted and turned, lost altitude, and shot back up again. As he fought to get the helicopter level, Rachel hung precariously from the door, her legs dangling in empty space. Her knuckles turned white with the effort of holding her weight. So strained with the effort, she couldn't make a sound.

Her fingers started to slip.

The helicopter finally leveled as Dawson managed to find the horizon. Then he quickly maneuvered the helicopter to an angle leaning toward the pilot's side. As her feet pumped the air, they finally connected with the landing skid, the bar running along the bottom of the helicopter. Supporting her weight on the bar, she then carefully transferred her hands one at a time to the interior seat. Her muscles weak and shaky from fear and fatigue, she still managed to pull herself up, hoisting one leg up and climbing in. Dawson stretched out his hand, grasping hers and helped pull her back in. Reaching out for the door handle once more, she grabbed it and slammed it shut.

Suddenly, the helicopter faltered again, rocking in a wide arc and knocking Rachel around like a pinball before she had time to put her seatbelt on. She felt pain explode in her head as she was flung against the now closed window.

She didn't know if she lost consciousness; she was just aware of Dawson calling her name over and over as if from a long distance.

"Rachel… Rachel. Come on. Talk to me."

When he reached over and rubbed his hand along her arm, she stirred, sitting up slowly and mechanically drawing her seatbelt across her body.

"Rachel, are you okay?

"I think so," she responded, taking mental inventory of her body. "Just a really bad headache."

"Rachel, you've got to be more careful!" Dawson said angrily.

Rachel looked at him sharply. What a ridiculous statement! Of course she was being careful! She was about ready to tell him so and include a few angry accusations of her own when she noticed his hands shaking as they worked at piloting the helicopter. She hadn't ever noticed his hands shake when they had been in dangerous situations before. He had always seemed so calm. Had he actually been afraid... for her?

Not waiting for a response, Dawson activated the radio. "This is Dawson Tate. The bomb has been exploded above the water." He gave coordinates for the blast. "We are returning to New York. The helicopter is damaged and difficult to control. I need to know the nearest place I can land."

"Tate, you're alive?" the voice said.

"Of course I am. I'm talking to you, aren't I? I think we managed to explode the bomb above the surface of the water, but I can't be sure. You should probably check satellite feed and be on the lookout for increasing water levels."

"We caught the explosion on satellite, but I didn't think you'd made it. I'm looking forward to your full report." The voice then gave Dawson coordinates for a landing site.

" Oh, and we'll need a medical team on the scene," Dawson added.

"Roger that."

As he ended the transmission, Rachel looked him over carefully. "Why is a medical team needed. Are you hurt?"

"No, you are. You hit your head pretty hard. And that's the second time. Remember the taxi wreck?"

"Just give me some aspirin and I'll be fine."

"You're going to get checked out anyway." His tone left no room for discussion.

"What about the helicopter? It's damaged? Will we make it?"

"We'll make it. I just have to make adjustments for whatever keeps pulling us off center."

"I'm sorry, Dawson. If I had managed to get the suitcase out the door with twenty seconds left, maybe we would have had enough clearance to not be impacted by the blast."

"No, Rachel, you did great. It wasn't the blast that got us. It was a massive air disturbance caused by the explosion--like an insanely strong gust of wind. I wasn't sure on the altitude. If you had gotten it out earlier, it may have detonated underwater. It was a long shot to begin with. The fact that we're alive and the helicopter has minimal damage is a miracle."

They both were silent for the next few minutes. Rachel's entire body began shaking uncontrollably. She kept silent, realizing by the helicopter's frequent jerks toward the pilot's side that it was requiring a lot of concentration and effort to keep it under control. Dawson was probably so focused that he didn't even notice her significant tremors.

It didn't take long before they were landing on the top of a building in Lower Manhattan.

The second the helicopter touched down, Rachel's door was yanked open and a man was reaching in to remove her bodily from the helicopter.

"Miss Saunders, you need to come with us right now."

Chapter 11

Rachel slid to the concrete. The man took hold of her upper arm and began leading her away from the helicopter. Rachel turned, looking around frantically for Dawson.

"Holmes, wait!" Dawson called, jogging up.

"Tate, we have to get her out of sight."

"I understand," Dawson replied. "But she's in shock. She most likely has a concussion."

"She'll be taken care of. You need to go give your report to…"

"Me." An older man and a younger woman joined them. The older man was tall, balding, and wearing a suit. By the air of respect his presence seemed to command from others, Rachel realized he was the man in charge.

"Well, Tate," the man said, "since you managed to detonate the bomb in a way that caused no damage, I guess I can overlook the fact that you disobeyed my order to die."

"I would appreciate that, sir," Dawson replied, smiling slightly. Rachel recognized the man's voice from the helicopter radio, but this was the most respectful Rachel had heard Dawson since she met him.

"So the explosion had no effect on Manhattan?" Dawson asked.

"None. We reviewed the satellite feed. It was as you said. The explosion was sizeable, but it occurred right above the water and too far away from land to cause any damage. We need to get your full report right away, though. We're still working to sort out all the pieces of this terrorist plot."

"Fine. And Miss Saunders...?" Dawson asked, indicating Rachel.

"Holmes, she shouldn't even be out here," the bald man said to Rachel's escort, obviously annoyed. "You were ordered to take her below immediately."

"Yes, sir, I..."

"Miss Johnson," he said, turning to the young woman at his side. "See if you can assist Mr. Holmes in completing his assignment. You will be handling Miss Saunders anyway."

Miss Johnson moved to Rachel's other side and began walking toward the door.

"Kelsey," Dawson called. Miss Johnson turned without pausing her stride. "Make sure she gets some medical treatment ASAP, okay?"

"Don't worry, Dawson. I'll take care of it."

"Thanks." Dawson turned toward his boss, ignoring the evil glares Holmes was sending his direction.

Once through the door on the roof, Rachel was led to an elevator. She was then taken to a small room with no windows and told to sit in a chair. The man called Holmes left immediately.

"Miss Saunders," Miss Johnson said. "May I call you Rachel?"

"Sure, and you are?"

"I'm an agent with Homeland Security, like Dawson Tate. Just call me Kelsey."

She certainly didn't look like Rachel's idea of an agent. She was young, probably a few years older than Rachel, and petite. Her hair was long and black, pulled back in a ponytail. Her skin was pale, her features delicate. Rachel thought she looked exactly like Snow White.

"Just sit tight a minute, Rachel. I'm going to run and get the doctor."

Kelsey left but was soon back with an aging doctor. He might have been a robot for as much bedside manner as he showed. Rachel was still shaking uncontrollably, yet he said not a word as he examined her, listening to her heart, taking her pulse, listening to her lungs, examining her eyes.

"Did you lose consciousness?" he finally asked.

"I'm not sure," Rachel replied honestly. "It's all kind of fuzzy. I have a pretty bad headache."

"You were also exposed to some smoke?"

"Yes."

"Still having bouts of coughing?"

It really hadn't occurred to Rachel until he asked, but, now that she thought about it, she was still having frequent moments of coughing and breathlessness. She realized that Dawson had been having similar episodes too, but they had both been so focused on survival, it hadn't even registered until now.

"I guess so," she replied

Completed with his examination, the doctor stood, walked to the door, and addressed Kelsey.

"She's in shock. She's dehydrated. She has a concussion. I don't think it's severe enough to warrant further tests. She has also had some significant smoke inhalation. Some oxygen will probably do her some good. Other than that, she needs rest and fluids. When she's asleep, see that she's woken up every few hours. I'll have some medication for the headache and some oxygen sent in."

The doctor left, and Kelsey turned back to Rachel.

"I know you're exhausted and feel terrible, Rachel. I wish I could just send you to bed. But, it's very important that I get your statement about what happened tonight. Something you say may provide some clues to this investigation."

"I understand. What do you need to know?"

Kelsey pulled out some paper, pen, and a recording device and set them on a table.

"I need to know everything."

The door opened and Holmes came in with an oxygen tank, several bottles of water, and a bottle of pills. After Rachel took the medication and got situated, Kelsey sat down across from her. She pushed the record button.

"Start when you first arrived at the airport," she instructed.

Rachel obediently related all of the night's events. She felt a little strange talking with oxygen tubes resting in her nostrils, but she just wanted to get this over with. Although she mentioned Dawson kissing her in front of her hotel (she didn't figure she could leave that out), she skipped over the parts where he kissed her again then said he wasn't interested. She also didn't mention that she had threatened to kill him if he kissed her again.

She also glossed over some of the unimportant details of her own involvement, completely omitting the part where she shot out the rearview mirror of the terrorists' car and minimizing her role in the fight in the alley. She said only that after she managed to disarm the terrorist threatening her, Dawson shot the one whose weapon was pointed at him, and he was then able to take the other one captive.

It wasn't as if she was seeking to be dishonest or even overly humble. She was just tired and didn't want to deal with the disbelief and questions that would surely follow if she relayed her entire involvement. She also didn't feel that any of that was essential to the narrative or the case. She wasn't a

DHS agent, Dawson was. They weren't really interested in her, other than for her statement. So, she simply tried to focus on what they need to know about Dawson and his actions, which, all things considered, were remarkable and heroic at every turn. She tried to keep the narrative very factual, omitting her personal emotions and fear.

She ended with relaying how she pushed the bomb out, lost her balance, and managed to climb back aboard assisted by Dawson's skillful piloting. Finally, she fell silent. She noticed that, at some point, her body had finally stopped shaking.

Kelsey asked her a few questions and asked for full descriptions of the man who brought the suitcase to her in the airport and all the other terrorists she encountered.

"I think that's all for now," Kelsey said finally, pushing a button to stop the recording. "You did a good job, Rachel. Your statement was very concise yet thorough. I'll let you know if we need anything else from you."

"Could I ask a couple questions?" Rachel asked. At Kelsey's cautious look, Rachel rushed forward. "I don't understand how the bomb was activated when your people said they had fully disabled both it and the tracking device."

The door opened and Dawson came in the room, catching the tail end of Rachel's question.

"I'm sorry, Rachel," Kelsey replied. "I can't really discuss that. Everything about this case is highly classified."

"Oh, come on, Kelsey!" Dawson interjected. "She already knows way too much anyway. What's the harm in filling in a few of the details? I know that very question was one of the first things I asked Andrews."

Kelsey still looked unsure.

"Fine," Dawson replied, turning to face Rachel directly. "The only explanation DHS has come up with is that the bomb was specifically rigged so both tracking and remote detonation could not both be simultaneously disabled. If the tracking was deactivated, the remote detonation was available if needed, but if the remote detonation was disabled, the tracking would automatically turn on again. It really was an ingenious failsafe. That's why the terrorist didn't overreact when they lost track of the bomb after the nightclub. They knew we were working to disable remote activation. The minute we succeeded, they could track the bomb again."

"That's how they knew we were at the dock," Rachel said, putting the pieces together.

"Exactly. And when our guys saw that tracking was reactivated, they worked to turn it off again."

"And when they succeeded, the terrorists could once again remotely detonate it."

"Which of course they did," Dawson finished. "They couldn't risk having the technology and potential clues to their organization fall into our hands."

Dawson turned to Kelsey. "Are you done with her now, Kelsey? I talked to the doctor. She needs some rest."

"We're done," she replied. "I just need to check with Andrews to make sure the arrangements have been finalized. Then I can take her to the hotel."

"I already checked with Andrews. I'm going to escort her to the hotel. You're supposed to check in with him, take care of a few details, and meet us there."

"She's my assignment, Dawson," Kelsey said, with a touch of iron lacing her voice.

"Andrews is sending both of us. I already discussed it with him."

"Dawson..." Kelsey said, disapproval in her tone. Something that Rachel didn't understand passed between the two agents. "Fine. I'll check with Andrews. Rachel, I'll meet you at the hotel shortly."

Kelsey walked out the door.

Gently Dawson removed the oxygen and unplugged it. "Kelsey will bring this and anything else you need. Let's get you out of here."

Dawson guided her back to the elevator, down to a parking garage, and into a waiting car.

"Did the doctor check you out too?" Rachel asked.

"Yes. I'm fine."

Rachel doubted that was the whole story, but she also doubted she would get any more information out of him.

"I have no idea what time it is. Do you think the hotel kept my reservation even though I didn't check in last night?

"It's about 8:00 in the morning," Dawson replied. "And you're not going to the InterContinental Times Square anyway."

They left the parking garage, Rachel seeing Manhattan bathed in full morning light. She had completely lost track of time and felt both surprised that so much time had passed and surprised that so much had happened in such a short amount of time.

"Why am I going to a different hotel?"

Dawson sighed, as if reluctant to answer her question. "You're still in danger, Rachel. We're taking you to a different hotel where Kelsey and I will keep you safe."

Dread settled like a rock in the pit of her stomach. "The bomb is gone. The terrorists have been apprehended. Why would I still be in danger?"

"We can't be certain that we have all of the terrorists. These terrorist rings can be massive with players on many different levels. The investigation is still ongoing. Although you were chosen randomly to be the mule, you can be certain that at least your name and picture will have been distributed, especially since you disappeared with the bomb."

"But the bomb is gone," Rachel repeated. "There's nothing left. Why would they still be after me?"

"Not everyone in the organization may realize the bomb has been detonated. Although the explosion was visible from shore, it happened early in the morning and the DHS has been able to keep it out of the media. The terrorists know you aren't a government agent, but they might also want you for information you could give them about our operations and their colleagues that have been apprehended."

"So how long will it take before I'm safe? I'm only supposed to be here for the weekend. My flight leaves on Monday. I would like to have at least part of my weekend in New York." Rachel knew that she was probably sounding somewhat desperate, like she was grasping at straws. But, at this point, she wanted to completely forget the past fifteen hours or so and enjoy her weekend, pretending that none of this had happened.

"I'm sorry, Rachel, that won't be possible. I'm taking you to a hotel so you can rest, recover, and get cleaned up. After which you will have to take an immediate flight home."

Rachel looked at Dawson, shocked. He was completely serious. She closed her eyes and took a deep breath. She realized there was nothing she could do.

"Will I still be in danger in Montana? Will they follow me back home?" She asked practically.

"We don't think so. This terrorist ring has already taken a big hit. By the time you're back home, we will have made even more progress in the investigation. They won't have the means or the need to follow you. Besides, we don't believe they have that much information about you. Everything through the hotel and travel agency says you're from Helena, but you aren't actually, right?

Our ranch is a ways outside of Helena," Rachel said. "That's just the city we're closest to and where my flight originated."

"We wouldn't be sending you home without protection if we had any reason to believe you to be in danger. Once you're out of New York, you'll be safe."

Turning into another parking garage, Dawson found an open spot by the elevator, parked and got out. Getting into the elevator, Dawson pressed the button for the fifth floor.

"Don't I need to check in at the front desk?" Rachel asked.

"You're already checked in. Under a different name, of course. I have the key to your room. Kelsey will have the other one."

Arriving on the fifth floor, they walked to room 523, and Dawson slid the key card into the door. It opened to reveal a very nice, large suite complete with a sitting room and two bedrooms on opposite ends.

"There are bathrooms connected to each of the bedrooms," Dawson explained. "You can pick which room you want. You've got to be hungry. I'll order some room service for us. You can get cleaned up when Kelsey arrives. She'll be bringing you some clothes and other things. Then you can go to bed. Sleep as long as you want."

"You've got to be just as exhausted as I am, Dawson. You need to sleep too."

He shrugged. "I will. Either Kelsey or I will be keeping watch while you sleep. While she's on duty here in the sitting room, I'll get some shut-eye in the other bedroom."

"I don't care which room I have as long as it has a bed. I guess I'll just take this one." Rachel moved toward the door of the closest bedroom."

"Rachel," Dawson called, his voice sounding strange. She turned around. "I need to thank you. You saved my life more than once last night."

Rachel was embarrassed. She didn't want his thanks. She felt herself blushing and looked at the floor, away from the sincere, almost vulnerable, blue eyes looking at her.

"Twice I had a gun trained on me with the terrorist ready to pull the trigger. I had no chance of getting away. And yet twice you managed to step in and save my life. In the alley and at the dock, you were more skilled than any agent I've ever worked with. For Pete's sake, Rachel! You shot the guy's gun hand! In the dark!"

Rachel shrugged. "Don't make me more heroic than I am. I probably should have shot the guy in the head. I had the shot. But, I just didn't know if I could pull the trigger on a kill shot like that. It was risky, but I was fairly certain I could hit his gun hand. I hoped that, if I missed, I could at least provide you with a distraction."

Dawson stepped forward slowly. Gently, he lifted Rachel's chin up with his finger so she was forced to meet his eyes.

"You were perfect, Montana. I couldn't have done it without you."

His eyes caressed her face.

"Rachel Saunders," he whispered. "You are thoroughly incredible."

The door to the hotel room opened. Dawson's hand dropped, and he swiftly stepped away.

"Rachel, I have some clothes and other toiletries so you can feel human again," Kelsey said, bustling in cheerfully.

"I'll order some food," Dawson announced, moving toward the phone.

Kelsey carried some bags into the bedroom and spread things out for Rachel to see: a soft nightgown, shampoo and conditioner, lotion, toothbrush and paste, jeans, sneakers, and a blouse.

Rachel was suddenly very self-conscious about how she looked. She had nearly forgotten that she was still dressed in her hooker outfit. Seeing the new clothes made her feel filthy and realize that she probably looked absolutely frightful. She self-consciously touched her long matted hair. Kelsey was beautiful and dressed so fashionably. At her very best, she didn't feel she could compare. No wonder Dawson said he wasn't interested in her.

"I hope I got everything," Kelsey said, oblivious to Rachel's internal self-torture. "I had to guess at the sizes. Just let me know if there's anything else you need and maybe I can run out and grab it while you're sleeping."

"Kelsey, Dawson is exhausted too," Rachel said quietly. "Couldn't they have assigned another agent as protection so he could recover?"

Kelsey looked at Rachel sharply. "They tried. But Dawson wouldn't let them. It was originally supposed to be only me, but Dawson insisted that you were his responsibility. This isn't the first time he's acted like this. He tends to get obsessive about his cases, insisting that he be the one to handle every last detail, tie up every loose end. He won't consider himself off duty until you're safely out of New York."

So it wasn't some affection that made Dawson want to stay and protect her.

"I see every mission through to the end," Dawson said, startling both women as he entered the bedroom. He had apparently heard at least part of Kelsey's response. "You're part of that mission, Rachel, so you're not going to get rid of me until I'm sure you're safe."

Part of his mission. That's all. Just one last detail that needed to be tended to.

There was a knock at the front door.

"That's got to be the food," Dawson said. "They said they were sending it right up."

Rachel and Kelsey followed him back into the sitting room. Checking the keyhole first, Dawson then opened the door and let in a dark-haired woman pushing a room service cart.

"Where would you like this, Sir," the woman asked with an accent Rachel didn't recognize.

"Right there by the couch would be great. Thank you."

"Hope you enjoy your food," she said, making eye contact with Kelsey and Rachel as well before leaving.

"Here, Rachel," Dawson said, handing her a plate. "You've got to be starved too. I just ordered a variety from their breakfast buffet. I can't even remember the last time I ate."

Dawson piled his plate high with bacon, eggs, and pancakes.

Rachel tried to summon up some enthusiasm but couldn't. She should have been famished, yet her stomach turned at the thought of a huge meal. Not wanting to appear ungrateful, she put a muffin, some bacon, and some hash browns on her plate. She forced herself to eat one piece of bacon and part of the muffin. Then she just sat there looking at her food, unable to take one more bite. As if sensing her quandary, Kelsey took her plate from her.

"Why don't you go in and get your shower now, Rachel?" she urged. "While you're doing that, I need to run and check in with Andrews." To Dawson, she said, "He decided that, since you're going to be here, I needed to finish the paperwork on Rachel's statement. I'll also be briefed on the progress of the investigation. I'll probably be gone about an hour or so, then I'll be back and you can get some sleep."

"That's fine," Dawson said. "I'm feeling great now that I've eaten something. Those pancakes are really good."

"With as hungry as you are, you'd probably think shoe leather tasted good too," Kelsey said, rolling her eyes.

"Sleep well, Rachel," Kelsey called as Rachel shut the bedroom door.

Rachel moved to the bed to collect the things she needed for her shower. She gathered the nightgown, a brush, and the shampoo and conditioner in her hands, but instead of moving toward the bathroom, she sat down on the bed. She gazed unseeingly at the items in her hands. Her mind began going through all the events since she arrived in New

York. All the scenes replayed in front of her eyes. All the danger and fear suffocating in its intensity. She began rocking back and forth as wave after wave of trauma washed over her. She had kept calm and sane through unimaginable events, never shedding a single tear. But now that dam burst, and her body convulsed in deep sobs.

So consumed in her nightmares, her consciousness barely registered the opening of the bedroom door. Strong hands took the things out of her hands, set them on the floor, and then bent low to remove her hooker boots. The mattress moved with the weight of another body sitting down beside her. Gentle arms drew her close, pulling her into a man's lap, and cradling her against a muscled chest. Soothing fingers smoothed her hair, wiped her tears. Tender lips trailed light kisses along her forehead. Warm breath whispered words of comfort.

"Ssshhhh. It's okay. It's all over. I'm here."

Dawson.

Chapter 12

Rachel woke slowly. The first thing she was aware of was the smell. What was that awful odor? Then, as her senses became more alert, she realized the truth: she stunk. She hadn't noticed it last night, but now, nestled between the clean sheets, the scent of smoke that permeated her entire body, her hair, her clothes, was inescapable.

With the smell came all the memories. She had intended to shower and hopefully wash some of those memories away with the filth before going to bed. But she hadn't made it that far. She remembered breaking down and sobbing uncontrollably, releasing all the pent-up fear and trauma. She remembered Dawson coming to her and holding her close while she cried. After falling asleep in his arms, he must have tucked her into bed.

She remembered his gentle caresses, his sweet kisses, his soothing words. Maybe he did care for her.

He wouldn't have done all that for her if she really was only a loose end in his mission, right?

Rachel sat up and scooted out of bed. She had the strong desire to head straight for the shower, but more overpowering was the need to see Dawson. She walked to the bedroom door and opened it a crack. She only wanted to see him. She really didn't want him to see and smell her the way she was now. Maybe if she could reassure herself that he was still here, that would reaffirm that her memories of his tender care were real. Then she could go get cleaned up and presentable.

Though she had tried to be quiet, the second the door opened, Kelsey turned around on the couch and looked directly at Rachel peeking through the door. Giving up, Rachel opened the door wide and walked into the sitting room. Dawson also looked up from where he was sitting in a chair looking at some papers. But, even before he made eye contact, he went back to his papers, as if completely disinterested in her presence.

"Hi, Rachel," Kelsey greeted. "How are you feeling?"

Rachel suddenly had a vague memory of Kelsey coming in several times while she was sleeping and trying to wake her. She had never fully awakened, but Kelsey had apparently been satisfied enough with her response to leave her alone.

"I'm fine," Rachel responded. "I still have a headache, but not bad. How long did I sleep? What time is it?

"It's about 6:00 in the evening," Kelsey answered. "You got about eight hours."

"I could probably sleep another eight, but I was awakened by my own stench. I guess I never made it to the shower."

"No," Kelsey said. "Dawson said you were too exhausted and never made it into the bathroom. I don't blame you. After what you'd been through, it was amazing you stayed upright as long as you did."

Rachel looked at Dawson, but he seemed to be completely ignoring her and their conversation. It didn't appear that Dawson had told Kelsey about her complete breakdown. She appreciated that. Of course she would rather Dawson hadn't been there to witness her weakness either, but that couldn't be helped. She might even think his omission was sweet. But, his current attitude of completely snubbing her was doing nothing to reinforce the idea of him being remotely sweet or considerate. Maybe he'd been so thoroughly disgusted by her and her emotional display that he wanted nothing to do with her now.

"I need to run and get done those things we talked about, Kelsey," Dawson announced, suddenly standing up. "I'll also have some food sent up."

"Sure," Kelsey replied. "After you get back, I'll trade off with you and see to the details of getting Rachel on the plane."

"Okay."

Dawson turned and walked to the door, never once looking at or addressing Rachel in any way. It was as if she was invisible to him. Completely flabbergasted, she turned to Kelsey to see if she had noticed Dawson's strange behavior. But the look on Kelsey's face stopped any question Rachel may have asked. As Dawson went out the door, she saw Kelsey watching him with a look that could only be described as longing.

The door clicked shut, and the look was gone. Kelsey turned to Rachel with a smile, as if that particular emotion had never crossed her face. Kelsey was so professional and friendly. If Rachel hadn't seen the expression herself, she would never have even believed it had been there.

Rachel sat down across from Kelsey, in the chair vacated by Dawson.

"Kelsey, do you mind if I ask you a personal question?" Rachel asked, deciding to be direct. After today, she'd probably never even see Kelsey again. What did she have to lose?

Kelsey looked cautious, but said, "Go ahead."

"I saw the way you looked at Dawson when he left. Are you and he involved romantically in some way?"

"No," Kelsey replied. "Dawson and I have never been involved romantically. We're colleagues, friends, but that's it. The look you saw... I guess I can't deny it. I'd be lying if I said I wouldn't like to be romantically involved with him."

"Does he know how you feel?" Rachel asked.

"No, probably not. But I know there's nothing I can do about it. Trust me, I'm not alone. I think every single woman who has contact with Dawson Tate has some manner of crush on the man. In fact, I'd wager that with the experiences you've had with him, you're probably half in love with him yourself, Rachel. That's what usually happens with the women he deals with on cases."

Rachel said nothing, but she felt a blush starting to seep into her cheeks.

"Don't be embarrassed, Rachel. Most of the women in our department have their sights set on Dawson, and, like I said, women who are involved in his cases seem especially susceptible to his charms. Not that he ever seems to purposely lead women on or even invite that interest. He's always been very professional and clear about boundaries as far as I can tell."

"So he never gets involved with any of the many women who are interested in him?"

"No, he doesn't, and I should probably warn you about that. It won't do you any good to let your heart harbor any hope of a relationship with Dawson. He has very strict personal rules. He never gets involved with women from work or from cases he works on. I've heard him mention it several times in passing to other colleagues."

"I understand," Rachel replied, clearly remembering when he 'mentioned' it to her as well. "So, since his rules apply to work, does he date outside of work?"

"If I remember right, I think he had a girlfriend who lived in Florida a few years back, but I have no idea if they're still together. Dawson keeps his personal life personal, but I certainly haven't heard of him going on a lot of dates. He's not a player at all. In fact, I think he's pretty religious. He's a Christian and seems to take his faith and convictions very seriously."

As if the man didn't have an aggravatingly perfect resume already, now Rachel found out for sure that they shared a faith. Not that it did her any good at this point.

"Thank you for being open with me, Kelsey. I already knew Dawson managed his personal life with some strict rules. I also knew that he had absolutely no romantic interest in me. But, I guess it's nice to know it's not just me."

"On the contrary, Rachel, while Dawson may not think of you romantically, he definitely thinks very highly of you. We were talking while you were sleeping. You played a lot bigger role in events than you let on in your statement. Dawson was very impressed, and, from what he told me, I am completely in awe of you. He said if you hadn't been there, he would have been dead on at least two separate occasions."

Rachel shrugged. "I guess I did what I had to do. Dawson saved my life too."

"Okay, but I need to know. Is it all true? Did you shoot the rearview mirror out of the terrorist's vehicle as Dawson swung around a curve? Did you escape and disarm a terrorist who had a gun to your head? Did you really shoot the gun hand of another terrorist who was about to shoot Dawson? And do it in the dark? Oh, and what was this about throwing your wig in someone's face and completely beating up another guy who tried to stop you from getting in the helicopter?"

Rachel grimaced. "I didn't realize Dawson even saw those last parts on the dock. I don't know that throwing my wig in the guy's face was one of my finer moments. I was just desperate at that point."

"Rachel, seriously, do you want a job? Dawson would probably kill me for asking, but, after reviewing the reports, especially Dawson's, Andrews asked me to feel you out a little bit. We could really use someone like you with Homeland Security. You would be very well compensated."

"Thank you, Kelsey. I'm flattered. But no. I just don't think I'm cut out for the kind of work you and

Dawson do. I think I'll be much happier back home on my family's ranch."

"I understand. But why don't you go ahead and give it some thought. The offer still stands, and there's not really an expiration on it. I'm sure Andrews would love to have you at any time."

"Thanks, Kelsey. I really appreciate everything. But, if you'll excuse me, I'm going to go get that much-needed shower. I just can't stand myself a second longer."

"Go for it. Who knows, you might even get that extra eight hours of sleep if they can't get you on a plane until morning. While you're showering, I'll check to see if Dawson already ordered us some food or if I need to get that done. I might not be here when you get out. As soon as Dawson comes back to take my place, I need to go take care of some details."

Rachel didn't know if anything in her entire life had felt as heavenly as that shower. It had been wonderful to peel off the icky hooker clothes and step into the hot water that eased her tense muscles and cleaned away the grime. It was like finally getting a nice hot shower after days on a dirty camping trip, but it was even better. She took her time, and, when she finally turned the water off, the bathroom was filled with steam. She hadn't bothered to turn on the vent. She couldn't stand the noise when she was trying to relax.

She pulled aside the curtain and reached for her towel. Before she could fully dry off and wrap her towel securely around her body, the bathroom door opened. A dark haired woman entered. She had a gun in her hand. And she pointed it directly at Rachel's chest.

Chapter 13

"Who are you?" the woman demanded.

Shocked and speechless, Rachel didn't know how to respond. As the steam in the bathroom lessened, she was able to recognize the woman as the same one who delivered their room service this morning.

"I said, WHO ARE YOU?" the woman asked again, this time more fiercely. "Answer me!"

"I don't know what you mean," Rachel finally answered. "I'm Rachel Saunders."

The woman shook her head as if that wasn't the answer she was looking for. Trying another tactic, she asked, "What do you know about the bomb?"

"I still don't know what you mean," Rachel answered. "The bomb is gone. It was detonated. I know nothing."

An angry look consumed the woman's face. "Stop playing stupid. You know what I want. If you're

not going to answer my questions, then I may as well just kill you."

Rachel was still standing in the tub. There was nowhere for her to go, and the side of the tub stood in her way for having a decent chance of disarming the woman. She would be dead before she even cleared it.

"Please," Rachel said. "I don't know what you want."

The woman smirked and leveled the gun directly at Rachel's heart. The range was so close she could see her finger adjust on the trigger.

"Drop the gun!" Dawson's voice rang from outside the bathroom.

The woman didn't move.

"Unless you want to die right now, put the gun down!"

Uncertainty and fear crossed her face. Then, slowly, she bent down and set the gun on the linoleum.

Dawson came up from behind and handcuffed her.

Rachel, shivering, tried to adjust her towel to gain the most coverage.

Dawson looked up at Rachel, his blue eyes intense. "Get dressed."

As soon as they left, Rachel finished toweling off and dressed quickly in the new clothes Kelsey had brought. She looked in the mirror just long enough to brush her wet hair. She noted that her eyes still looked big and frightened, her skin pale.

Rushing out to the sitting room, she arrived just as some other men were taking custody of the dark-haired woman and leading her away. The door closed. Dawson turned and looked at Rachel. He was silent. Slowly, he crossed the room to her, his intense eyes never leaving her face. He stopped two feet away and broke eye contact.

"I'm sorry, Rachel. I let her in. She was bringing the food. When she came in, she said the hotel had provided fresh flowers for the room. She asked if I wanted her to place them in the bedroom. I let her. I knew you were taking a shower and figured you'd enjoy the flowers. I started eating when I suddenly realized I didn't hear your shower running anymore. She'd been gone too long. I'm sorry. I was so stupid."

"No, Dawson, you didn't know. She had been in here last night with no problem. There was no way you could have predicted this. You still managed to save my life."

Dawson moved forward. Gently he cupped her cheek in his hand. Rachel shut her eyes, her skin tingling at his touch. Brokenly, he whispered, "If I had been just a few seconds later..."

They heard the beep of the door unlocking a second before it was flung open. Kelsey flew into the room.

"Dawson, what happened? Rachel, are you okay?"

Rachel nodded.

At Kelsey's entrance, Dawson had dropped his hand and moved away, though not with the same urgency as when Kelsey had previously entered unannounced.

Dawson explained, "The same hotel employee from this morning brought our food again. She asked to put some flowers in Rachel's bedroom, and then she pulled a gun on Rachel as she was finishing her shower. I know, Kelsey. I should have never let her go into that bedroom."

"What was her motive?" Kelsey asked, ignoring Dawson's remorse.

"We don't know yet. Our orders are to remain here until they interrogate her and figure out if it's safe for Rachel to leave."

Kelsey turned to Rachel. "Did she say anything to you, Rachel? Did she say what she wanted?"

"What she said didn't make sense. She asked who I was and what I knew about the bomb. She seemed to think I already knew what she wanted. When I couldn't answer in the right way, she didn't believe me. She said she'd just kill me if I didn't give her the information she needed."

"I guess we'll just have to wait to make sense of it after we hear the report from the interrogation. We'll order some new food, just to make sure it's safe. You can finish getting ready, Rachel."

Rachel moved to return to her bedroom, but not before she saw Kelsey place a reassuring hand on Dawson's forearm.

"Dawson, don't beat yourself up over it," Kelsey said quietly. "Hindsight is 20/20. We all have regrets, things we wish we would have seen sooner. You just have a lot less than the rest of us. You're not used to it."

By the time Rachel had dried her hair, fixed it, and applied some makeup, the food in the sitting room had been replaced. Despite the most recent ordeal, Rachel was starving. This time she piled her plate high with a large variety of the Mexican food on the cart and ate every bite.

As she was finishing up, both Kelsey and Dawson received simultaneous calls on their cell phones. Apparently, not wanting to give the report twice, their boss did a conference call so both agents could hear. Hanging up, they turned to Rachel.

"You're all cleared to get out of here, Rachel," Kelsey said. "Final arrangements are being made. We'll take you to the airport and get you on a flight back to Montana. Sorry, but you'll probably have to sleep on the plane. You'll be taking a red-eye."

"Did they interrogate the woman?" Rachel asked. She wasn't going to let them get by without sharing what they learned about her attacker. "What did they find out?"

"She was the wife of one of the terrorists arrested on the dock," Dawson answered. "Our theory is that she recognized you this morning and waited around for the opportunity. The hotel reported that she traded another worker so she could work a double shift today. We're still not sure what she expected to get from you. But, she was probably desperate and trying to find out any information that would help free her husband."

"The terrorist ring is in pieces," Kelsey said. "As soon as you're out of New York, those pieces won't come after you. You'll be safe."

"I guess I'm ready whenever," Rachel said. "It's not like I have anything to pack."

"Alright," Kelsey said. "I'm going to go on ahead and make sure security and everything is ready at the airport. You still have a little time. Dawson will drive you when he gets the official green light."

Kelsey left. Dawson sat on the couch, silent and engrossed in something on his phone. Rachel didn't feel like eating anymore. Finally, tired of Dawson ignoring her, she retreated to the bathroom to overanalyze her hair and makeup.

After only a few minutes, Dawson knocked on the bathroom door and said, "Time to go, Rachel."

Dawson's silence continued when they were in the car and on their way. It was once again dark when they left the hotel. An involuntary shiver ran through Rachel. She felt like she had skipped the daylight hours and landed right back at the time of day she most wanted to forget. The memories from last night were still too fresh. Her nerves once again came on alert, and she found that she kept expecting to hear gunfire around every corner.

The awkward silence with Dawson didn't help. Rachel fidgeted with her hands. She didn't know what to say. Should she try to make small talk? Start a conversation? She was leaving and she'd probably never see Dawson again. What was the point?

"Have you ever heard the statistics about relationships beginning at a highly stressful, emotional time?" Dawson suddenly broke the quiet.

Somewhat startled, Rachel answered, "I think I have. You mean like relationships started during a shared traumatic event?"

"Yes."

"They pretty much don't last," Rachel said. "There's an extremely high rate of breakup. Probably most relationships like that don't seem to last long because they're based on adrenaline and exaggerated emotion. After that fades and life returns to normal, the magic carriage turns back into a plain old pumpkin."

"Exactly."

Were they just making conversation and talking about statistics in general, or was Dawson referring to something a little more personal?

"And of course," Rachel inserted. "There are never any exceptions to those statistics. No couple who meets under extraordinary, highly-emotional circumstances ever stays together."

If Dawson was going to use veiled small talk instead of talking to her openly, then she would do her best to throw a veiled, sarcastic wrench into each one of his insane excuses!

"I've heard similar statistics on long distance relationships as well," Dawson said.

"You're right. They don't work either. No exceptions."

Dawson was silent.

The man was maddening! She was leaving and *this* is what he wanted to talk about!

"Dawson, now that I think about it, you're probably very wise to have all the rules you do about relationships." Then, counting the rules off on her fingers, Rachel listed, "Let's see, don't get involved with someone from work. Any woman remotely associated with any case is off limits too. Never build a relationship with a shared highly emotional experience. Long distance relationships are off limits too. Wow, Dawson, stick to those rules and you'll never get hurt! I mean, that's so smart. I've never even heard of any exceptions to those scenarios."

Dawson didn't say a word.

Rachel took a deep breath. She should probably lay off the sarcasm. She didn't want to upset him. She didn't even feel the need to show him the error of his ways. He didn't want a relationship with her. She got it. Message received. He really didn't need to parade all his reasons for her to feel better!

Rachel was just working up to forming some kind of an apology and attaching a dignified thank you for saving my life multiple times, but Dawson was pulling into the airport before she got the chance. Instead of pulling into parking at the terminal, he pulled around to a gate, showed his ID, and drove around the terminal and onto the tarmac.

"What are we doing?" Rachel asked.

"You aren't really taking a normal flight home, Rachel. We've made all the arrangements. You don't have to check in at the airport. In fact, there will never be a record of you on this flight. You will just disappear from New York. We thought it would be safer this way, given the very slim chance of you being tracked."

Dawson pulled up to some other cars and got out. Rachel followed suit. Kelsey, along with several other men, were standing around one of those small vehicles used to shuttle things around the tarmac.

"Everything's ready, Rachel," Kelsey said by way of greeting. "I took the liberty of purchasing you a new suitcase. After all, it was the least we could do after all you did. I put in the clothing and items that were left inside the helicopter. We also found some other items we assumed were yours when we searched the baggage claim area of the airport. I'm sure it wasn't everything that was taken from your original suitcase, but at least it's something."

"Thank you, Kelsey. I really appreciate it."

"Your suitcase has already been loaded on the plane," Kelsey said, indicating a plane that appeared to be taking on passengers a little ways away. "As I'm sure Dawson explained to you, there is no record of you on this flight. The plane will stop in Cincinnati, but you won't disembark. You will have a layover in Denver, but we have an agent who will meet you, keep you in a secure location, and get you on the new plane. When you arrive in Helena, you'll be on your own. Sorry about the late flight, but we figured it would be better this way. Try to get some sleep in the air."

"Thanks, Kelsey," Rachel repeated. "I really appreciate everything you've done for me."

"You're very welcome, Rachel. Oh, I do have to remind you that you cannot tell anyone anything about what went on here in New York. Everything is classified as top secret. The media knows nothing. It would be disastrous if any word got out that a terrorist attack had been so imminent. You are the only person without a high level clearance who knows anything about this. Do you understand?"

Rachel nodded, "I understand. I won't breathe a word."

She had no idea what she would tell her parents about returning early, but she'd figure out something. She instinctively knew that the toughest part was going to be dealing with the memories all alone.

"Alright then. Rachel, this agent is going to drive you over to the plane and get you settled."

Rachel moved to get on the transport vehicle.

"Oh, Rachel," she turned back around at Kelsey's voice. "Have you given any more thought to the job offer? Would you consider joining the Homeland Security team?

She was facing Dawson when Kelsey asked the question. She saw his eyes open wide as he shot Kelsey with an accusing glare.

"Kelsey…!" he growled.

"Dawson, this doesn't concern you!" she shot back at him.

Rachel was feeling emotionally exhausted once again and had no mental energy to analyze Dawson's reaction.

Instead, she simply answered the question. "No, Kelsey, I'm really not interested. Thanks for the offer though. It's very flattering."

Another agent walked up as Rachel moved to get on the transport.

"Dawson, Andrews is in the office upstairs. He wants to see you ASAP."

Dawson turned and walked away. The other agent drove Rachel to the plane and escorted her to her seat.

She was the last passenger to board, and the plane soon began to move. They lifted off. Rachel watched out the window as the lights of the airport and then the lights of New York quickly faded to indistinguishable dots, then darkness. It was then that she realized. Dawson hadn't even said goodbye.

Chapter 14

Rachel arrived in Helena, Montana at 9:00 AM. The flight home had both felt like it took forever and felt like it passed in a blur. What little sleep she'd gotten had been extremely restless and plagued by nightmares. The layover in Denver had been uneventful. Finally getting off the plane was a relief, but she still had to collect her suitcase, get her car, and drive herself home. Then, nothing was going to keep her from a long appointment with her bed. Maybe a very long nap would erase the memories enough for her to pretend the events of the past two days simply hadn't happened.

She made her way down to the luggage carousel flashing her flight number. Patiently, she waited as all the luggage from the plane danced around her and was claimed by other passengers. Finally, the carousel stopped moving, the flight numbers stopped blinking. She didn't know what the suitcase Kelsey had purchased for her looked like, but there was nothing left on the empty carousel for her even to inspect.

Groaning, Rachel went over to the Lost Luggage counter.

"Excuse me," she said to the middle-aged lady behind the counter whose nametag read 'Dawn.' "My name is Rachel Saunders. I was on the flight that just landed from Denver. I was supposed to have a suitcase on board, but it didn't show up on the carousel."

The sensation of déjà vu made Rachel feel sick to her stomach. Only this time, she didn't even have a ticket stub or a baggage claim ticket to prove that she'd been on the flight. Kelsey hadn't given her any papers, and there wasn't even a record that she'd been on the flight.

"Rachel Saunders?" Dawn asked. "Let me run in back and make sure there wasn't a suitcase that just didn't get loaded. If it's not there, we'll start some paperwork. Wait here. I'll be right back.

Rachel fought the urge to start laughing hysterically. This was not happening! Not again!

True to her word, Dawn came bustling back within two minutes.

"Good news!" she said "We found it! A man is bringing it out for you right now."

Rachel closed her eyes. This *really* wasn't happening! She didn't know if she could take it. Maybe she should just forget the suitcase and run!

She opened her eyes to see a mirage. Dawson was walking toward her. Had she finally lost it and gone insane?

The mirage came toward her, a small smile lifting the corners of his mouth, showing off his dimples. Before she could even think, his lips were on hers, kissing her slowly, tenderly, passionately. After a few seconds of complete shock, Rachel responded, placing her hands on his muscled chest and leaning in to fully enjoy every nuance of his mouth on hers. If this was a dream, she didn't want to wake up.

Breathless, the mirage finally released her. Reaching up, he tangled both hands in her hair and tipped her face up so her eyes met his.

"I don't want to give you the wrong impression, Montana," he said, his voice scratchy with emotion. "But I have to tell you I plan on making a habit of that."

Rachel, her brain fully muddled by his kiss, didn't follow. "A habit of what?"

"Of kissing you. Long, passionately, frequently. I like it. A lot. In fact, I'll probably do it just about any time I want."

Rachel shook her head. "You can't be real. The Dawson Tate I know doesn't like me. He doesn't like kissing me. He doesn't want to be romantically involved with me."

"Wow," Dawson said, rubbing his hand over his stubble. "I didn't think I'd managed to fool you. Of course I like kissing you. I enjoyed it the very first time in front of the hotel. From the very beginning, I cared for you way too much. I tried everything to fight against my attraction to you. I tried to push you away. But, in the end, I realized I couldn't let you go. You are the strongest, sexiest, bravest, most beautiful, nicest, most talented, most wickedly tough woman I've ever met. I couldn't let you disappear from my life."

"I still don't believe you," Rachel said stubbornly. "Dawson Tate has all these rules. 'No getting involved with women from cases, no relationships began under traumatic circumstances, no long distance relationships, no…"

Dawson gently grabbed Rachel's fingers as she assigned each of them a rule number and brought them to his lips. "I know my rules, Rachel." He paused and made sure she was looking directly into his eyes. "I guess I just found an exception."

Dawson's words finally hit their mark.

Rachel's throat was suddenly dry and breathless. *This* really couldn't be happening. Could it?

"Well, Hollywood," she said, trying to ignore the fluttering of her heart. "I know I said I'd kill you if you kissed me again, but... since you made an exception, I guess I can make one too."

"Thank you, I appreciate that," he said, bending and whispering in her ear. "Especially since I'm planning on taking my life into my own hands and thoroughly kissing you on a regular basis."

Gently, he feathered kisses along her ear and down her cheekbone, finally ending once again at her lips. After a few moments, he lifted his head again, breathing deeply.

"I guess I need to stop doing that if we want to make it out of the Lost Luggage department.

"Wait a minute!" Rachel said, suddenly coming to her senses. "How did you get here before me? You were talking to Andrews when my flight left."

"Did you forget who I work for? Homeland Security has their own planes, and I currently have hero status in the agency. It wasn't difficult. With your layover in Denver, I had plenty of time to spare."

Rachel stared at him wordlessly.

"Come on, Montana. Let's get out of here. You need to take me home so I can see your ranch and meet your parents."

"You really want to meet my parents?" That thought had never even occurred to Rachel.

"Of course I do. Rachel, you're stuck with me. I don't do casual relationships. It's all or nothing with me. Is that okay?"

Completely floored, all Rachel could do was nod. She still couldn't grasp the fact that he had chosen her. That he wanted to be with her.

"But how long can you stay? How are we going to manage a long distance relationship?"

Dawson grinned. "It just so happens that after my incredible girlfriend and I managed to save New York, I got a promotion. That's what Andrews wanted to talk to me about when you left. I was offered a position as head of a western branch of Homeland Security. I'll probably still have to travel and go on assignments, but, since DHS is everywhere, I can pretty much choose where I want to live. I'm open to suggestions. You can certainly submit your application on the matter."

Wordlessly, Rachel stood on her tiptoes and kissed him, loving the idea that she even had permission to do so, let alone that he obviously enjoyed it.

"I guess, when you put it that way…"

Dawson picked up two suitcases and a sack he'd dropped on the floor, and they started to walk toward the airport doors. Suddenly, Dawson stopped.

"Oh, here's your suitcase, Rachel. And don't worry, I already checked it. No bomb." He transferred the suitcase handle to Rachel and then opened the sack he carried. "Oh, and, Montana, you forgot theses at the hotel."

With an evil glint in his eye, he handed Rachel the all-too-familiar hooker boots.

Rachel thought through her options, one of which included beating him over the head with the stupid things. Finally, she accepted the boots, set them on the floor, reached up, and kissed him passionately.

When she eventually released him, she noticed with satisfaction that he was obviously a little disoriented and unsteady.

"What was that for?" he asked.

"You were breathing too heavily."

She picked up her boots and suitcase and walked out the door. Smiling and shaking his head, Dawson Tate followed.

**Please enjoy the following Sneak Peek of
Book 2...**

MiRAGE

Chapter 1

Rachel stared at the phone. It was going to ring any second. Dawson always called her at night when he was traveling. He'd never missed a night, not a single one. It's not like she insisted that he check in with her. He'd just started the habit of calling every night when he was away to check in and let her know he was okay.

The phone was silent. Rachel wasn't a worrier by nature, but, when your boyfriend is a top agent with Homeland Security and frequently works extremely dangerous cases, you tend to get a little concerned. While she had purposely never mentioned being afraid for him, Dawson had been intuitive and sweet enough to prevent much potential concern with a nightly update. Not that he ever told her anything about the cases he was working on. The man was like a high security vault when it came to his job. This fact aggravated Rachel to no end. She was curious, okay nosey, about Dawson's work, especially since she'd had a full dose of the danger involved six months ago when she'd become entangled in a terrorist plot involving a bomb in New York City. Rachel had escaped the encounter with her life, the knowledge that she had helped foil the plan and save lives, and one incredibly handsome Homeland Security agent as a boyfriend.

To her surprise, Dawson had joined her back in Montana, accepting a promotion that allowed him more flexibility. Although Dawson was now a supervisor, he still had to travel a lot more than Rachel had originally anticipated. She'd thought he'd be supervising the cases of other agents, not working so many himself.

Despite the fact that he was gone a lot and could never tell her anything about what he was working on, the last six months had been the best of Rachel's life. She knew, without a doubt, that she was absolutely, positively, completely head-over-heels in love with Dawson Tate.

Now if he would just call! The mute phone sat in its cradle blissfully ignorant of any task it was supposed to be performing. The red power light on the base was the only sign that it was even functioning. Rachel growled in frustration and flopped back on her bed. It was late, and she was already so tired from a long day of feeding cattle and checking fences in the Montana cold.

Dawson had never been this late in calling before. He had left early this morning. His flight had landed hours ago. The only thing she knew about this trip was that he was flying to Florida, which he seemed to do a lot lately. Florida's time zone was two hours later than Montana's. He should have already called her from his hotel and been in bed.

Rachel's exhaustion and frustration soon turned to anger. She was not the type of girl to wait by the phone for a guy to call, no matter what the circumstances. She sat up, grabbed the cordless phone off the cradle, and purposely pushed the buttons for Dawson's cell phone number. If he wasn't going to have the decency to call her and let her know that he was safe, then she was going to call him and voice her thoughts on the issue.

The call went through but went straight to voicemail, as if the phone was turned off. Rachel disconnected the call before the beep to leave a message. His phone would show her missed call whether or not she left a message.

Why would his phone be off? He never turned it off. He always had to be available for his job. Any conversation or activity could be interrupted at any time by Dawson's phone. And now it was off?

She suddenly felt a jolt of fear. It wasn't like Dawson not to call her, and it really wasn't like him to turn his phone off. In fact, she had never known him to do so. Rachel scooted off her bed and padded barefoot across the cold hardwood floor to her closet. Finding her coat, she rummaged around in the pocket for her own cell phone. Part of her didn't even know why she bothered. Dawson never called her on her cell phone at home. He knew she got terrible reception.

Dawson's phone, on the other hand, was almost like a star trek version of a cell phone; he got great reception wherever he was. Rachel knew the latest technology and the fact that it was a government issued and maintained phone had something to do with Dawson's stellar coverage. But, since she didn't have the option for *that* service provider, she simply had to continue with her rotten coverage and her slightly jealous hatred of Dawson's futuristic communication device.

Rachel's hand finally connected with the phone. She drew it out of the pocket and looked at it. No new messages. No missed calls.

Thoughtfully she took the cell phone back to bed and lay down. She had already showered and was in her most unflattering flannel pajamas. Her parents had gone to bed hours ago in their bedroom on the opposite side of the ranch house. Rachel laid both the cordless phone and her cell phone beside her on the bed.

There had to be a perfectly reasonable, safe answer for why Dawson hadn't called. Maybe he had lost his cell phone. Maybe something important had come up and he was tied up in a late night meeting.

But no matter how much she tried, no excuses shrank the stark fear lodged in the pit of her stomach. If Dawson had really been heading for a dangerous mission, surely he would have told her something or given her some kind of warning, even if he couldn't share the details, right?

The thoughts swirling around her head soon morphed into dreams. A man in a dark jacket stood a few feet away from Dawson, his extended hand holding a gun aimed directly at Dawson's head. Dawson was unarmed, helpless. Rachel could see the man's finger poised on the trigger. She screamed, but no sound came out. She tried to run to reach him, but something physically held her back. Her feet wouldn't move. The gun fired. Dawson fell as Rachel's screams echoed through the air and the entire scene dissolved before her eyes.

Now she was on a beach facing two figures caught in each other's arms as they stood in the foaming surf. Rachel moved forward, the sand warm on her bare feet as she was drawn like a magnet to the embracing couple. The man's face turned toward her. Dawson! He didn't seem to even notice Rachel's presence as his attention was completely focused on the beautiful brunette in his arms. He smiled, drawing her close once more and kissing her long and tenderly. A sob caught in Rachel's throat.

The first ring of a phone shattered the beach scene. Rachel's hand fumbled for the handset.

"Hello?" she managed, her voice still muddled with sleep.

"Hey, Rachel. It's Dawson. I'm sorry to wake you, Sweetheart, but I didn't want you to worry. I got redirected to New York. I'm so sorry I wasn't able to call you earlier, but I've been in an urgent meeting with Andrews. I couldn't call you sooner."

The simple sound of his voice blew away her anger and fear, leaving her weak and slightly speechless.

"I'm just glad to know you're okay," she finally said simply, deciding it would do no good to tell him how really scared she'd been.

"I need to let you get more sleep, but I'll call you in the morning and we can talk longer. Sleep well, Rachel. I love you."

At the sound of those three precious little words, Rachel bolted upright in bed. Her Dawson had never told her he loved her.

She looked around her bedroom, seeing the faint light of dawn breaking through the late winter sky and breaching the edges of the blue gingham curtains at her window. The two phones lay undisturbed on the mattress beside her. Rachel went from asleep to awake and panicking in a split second as two realizations hit her. One, it was morning. Two, Dawson had never called.

If you enjoyed this preview, MiRAGE, and other books by Amanda Tru may be purchased from the same online store where you purchased this book. Happy reading!

About the Author

Amanda loves to write exciting books with plenty of unexpected twists. She figures she loses so much sleep writing the things, it's only fair she makes readers lose sleep with books they can't put down!

Amanda has always loved reading, and writing books has been a lifelong dream. A vivid imagination helps her write captivating stories in a wide variety of genres. Her current book list includes everything from holiday romances, to action-packed suspense, to a Christian time travel / romance series.

Amanda is a former elementary school teacher who now spends her days being mommy to three little boys and her nights furiously writing. Amanda and her family live in a small Idaho town where the number of cows outnumbers the number of people.

You can find Amanda Tru on Facebook or at her website! She loves hearing from readers!

Facebook:
https://www.facebook.com/amandatru.author
Website:
http://www.amandatru.blogspot.com
Email:
truamanda@gmail.com